In Too Deep

~ Grayton Series ~
Roman & Marissa

Follow Jill online at:

Jill@JillSanders.com
http://JillSanders.com
Jill on Twitter
Jill on Facebook
Sign up for Jill's Newsletter

Summary

Roman has been searching for his long-lost adopted sister, Marissa. When she disappeared shortly after her seventeenth birthday, he was the only one who had a clue why.

Now that he's finally found out where she's been hiding all these years, he would do anything to get back the only woman he's ever loved.

by
Jill Sanders

Chapter One

Missy leaned against the counter and swayed her hips to the old tune that was pumping out of the small speakers she'd hung up the week before. The short shorts she was wearing were a little too old and loose, but she didn't care, not when the music was taking her back to the good ol' days.

Images flashed in her mind as she punched the keys to the old ten-key calculator. She smiled when she saw that she was under budget again this month, but she would work the numbers once more just to make sure.

It still got her deep in her chest when she saw the extra money sitting in her bank account after everything was paid at the end of the month. Smiling, she looked up as one of her employees, Jenny, walked in.

The girl was young and pretty enough to keep customers happy, even when they found out they would have to pay a little more than at some of the other places along the Gulf shore.

White-sugar-sand beaches sat right outside of Dog's Landing's front door, along with the long dock that housed three of her best moneymakers. One boat was a ferry, which could carry five full-size cars to Dog Island, along with over a dozen passengers. One of the other boats was smaller, but made just about as much money as the ferry did carrying parasailers across the crystal-clear waters of the Gulf. Her last boat was bigger and made the most money by taking a group of eight out into the deeper waters on fishing charters.

Buying the two other boats had been one of the first changes she'd made when she'd inherited the small convenience store, along with the dock and the old ferryboat.

It had been a shock at first, running her own business, but she'd adjusted, like she always had in life.

Sighing, she stood up and watched Jenny straighten a few cans of food and boxes of cereal as she made her way towards the back of the store.

Her long blonde hair swayed with each step she took. Her standard uniform of shorts and a button-up blouse made Missy remember she had wanted to go clothes shopping for a few new items.

"Sorry I'm late." Jenny smiled as she walked around the counter.

Missy laughed. "Jenny, you're never late." She glanced at the clock and smiled. "Actually, you're five minutes early."

Jenny sighed. "I'm late if I'm not ten minutes early."

Missy shook her head at her. "I just can't understand it."

Jenny leaned against the counter and giggled. "My granny taught me well."

"Wish I could say the same about all my other employees." She frowned when she noticed that the smallest of her boats was still docked outside. There were customers waiting out on the docks for their turn to enjoy flying over the water. "Where are Tom and Roger?" She sighed and knew it was past time to get more reliable employees to run the parasailing tours.

"Where do you think?" Jenny picked up the shop phone and dialed. "Hey, yeah, again." She rolled her eyes. "Okay. Thanks."

Missy crossed her arms over her chest and watched Jenny hang up the phone. "You can't keep asking them to do this."

Jenny smiled. “I know, but they like it.”

“He’s old. They’re too old.”

Jenny laughed. “Not as old as you think.”

“I don’t know how those two can keep up with people half their age.”

Jenny smiled and shrugged her shoulders. “They tell me working here keeps them young.”

Missy laughed. “Right.” Just then they both turned to see Jenny’s grandfather, John, and his best friend, Bob, walk in. Both men were in shorts and smiling from ear to ear.

The men lived less than a block from the store and had been a staple in both Carrabelle, Florida, and to Dog’s Landing since before she’d been born.

“Good thing you called. We were driving the wives stir-crazy.” Bob chuckled as he walked over and grabbed the boat keys from behind the countertop.

“Full day?” John asked.

She nodded. “You’re booked solid. Unless Tom and Roger show up, it’s all yours for the day.”

As the men glanced at each other then walked out chuckling, Jenny leaned closer. “You know they make more in tips than Tom and Roger.”

She sighed and nodded. “Yeah, it’s funny when two old men can out-earn two young hunks.”

Jenny laughed. "Tom and Roger are not hunks. They're dorks."

Missy frowned and tilted her head. "I wish you would have told me that when I hired them."

"I did." She laughed. "Trust me, next time, let me do the hiring."

She nodded. "Okay, it's all yours." There were still things she was learning about the business, even after five years of running it.

"I'm going to head out on the next ferry ride. I've got a few deliveries." She nodded to the cart full of boxes, which were stuffed with orders.

The store had many customers who lived on Dog Island in St. George Sound, one of Florida's only totally secluded islands. There was a small airstrip on the island, but most of the locals used her ferry service to move between the island and the mainland. Many of the people who lived on the island were pretty self-reliant. There were fewer than three dozen homes on the semi-private island and she had almost a dozen loyal customers who helped keep her doors open and her shelves stocked with groceries.

Dog's Landing had been delivering groceries to the islanders since she'd taken over the store. The customers loved that their food was delivered fresh daily and she loved the work.

"Enjoy it. I hear we're supposed to have some bad weather later this week." Jenny leaned down and pulled out a fresh bottle of water from the stocked fridge behind the counter.

"Yeah." She frowned. "Already I've had a few cancellations for fishing trips."

Jenny shrugged her shoulders. "I'll bet it will pass quickly. It always does this time of year. Then, you watch. We'll be booked solid for the Fourth of July."

Missy smiled as she loaded the small handcart full of the deliveries. "Yeah, remember last year?" She laughed. "The two groups that fought over the charter boat." She laughed, remembering how the two groups had tried to outbid one another for the day use of her boat.

"We could hire another boat this year," Jenny said, looking over the schedule book. "We're already booked, but I bet we could easily book another boat solid for that weekend."

She tilted her head. "Do you know someone?"

Jenny smiled. "I don't, but I bet my grandfather would. I can ask him when he comes in for lunch."

Missy thought about it and nodded. "While you're at it, if he knows anyone else to hire…"

Jenny laughed. "I'll ask. If Tom and Roger show up?"

She sighed and closed her eyes. "I guess I need to go ahead and rip that Band-Aid off as well."

Jenny smiled. "I'll do it. Don't worry. I already

have one person in mind for replacing them. I'll have to look around for another." She frowned.

"You are too good to me." Missy smiled. "I don't know what I would do without you."

"Good thing you pay me well." She smiled at their private joke. "Now, you'd better get going. The ferry is coming in." She nodded towards the front windows. Sure enough, the big boat was making its way towards the dock.

By the time Missy had carted out the two loads of boxes and the large cooler for her deliveries, the ferry was already filled up with new passengers and cars.

She waved up to Clay, one of the ferry captains. Clay and Marv, two men who had worked as ferry master for the past eight years, usually alternated workdays. She allowed them to make their own schedules, since it tended to work best when they communicated with one another directly. She didn't mind, so long as there was someone manning the ferry seven days a week.

She stored the supplies and locked them down for the half-hour journey to the island, and then she made her way up to sit next to Clay.

"Hey," she sighed as he started pulling the ferry away from the dock.

"Hey." He smiled over at her. Clay was easily one of the sexiest men she knew. But all the women around knew that Clay's wife of almost ten years, and his high school sweetheart, was eight and a half months pregnant. “Do you have a lot of deliveries today?” He glanced over at her quickly and she wished more than anything that she could find someone that would cause her heart to skip who didn’t have a gold band around his finger.

She shrugged her shoulders. “It might take me a while.” She rolled her eyes. “Mrs. Mette has two boxes today.”

He chuckled and she felt her insides kick at the rich sound. She could only ever remember one other person who’d caused her body to respond that way. Sighing, she forced her mind to focus as she glanced below deck at the passengers enjoying the slow ride.

“I don’t know why you let that woman push you around like she does.”

She smiled. “Well, it helps that she’s one of our best customers.”

Clay glanced at her again. “And one of the craziest people on Dog Island.”

She chuckled. “Yeah, but you have to admit, she give us something to talk about.”

He laughed and nodded and then focused on maneuvering the ferry out of the small port and into the deeper waters of Saint George Sound.

Missy loved the peaceful ride out to the island and back. She even enjoyed riding the small electric cart on the island to deliver the groceries.

She really did enjoy everyone on the island, even Mrs. Mette, although it was quite a pain when she happened to be in one of her moods.

Missy shivered at the thought of having to run back to the mainland to replace an item she wasn't satisfied with. One time, it had taken her a full day of running back and forth before Mrs. Mette was satisfied that she had the freshest eggs possible.

By the time she had everything unloaded from the ferry, with the help of Clay, there was a small trail of sweat rolling down her back. She loved living along the Gulf Coast, especially during the summer months.

As she pulled her small electrical cart out of the parking area, she waved at a few locals and hit the small road towards her first delivery. Dog Island was a small community she loved being part of, even though she didn't live on the island herself. She smiled as she pulled up to her first stop and thought of her small cottage a few blocks from the store. She'd been shocked when she'd found it up for sale and had been even more in shock when she'd been approved for the loan. She could remember the countless hours she'd spent as a child dreaming about her future home. This one hadn't disappointed her childhood dreams.

The first few deliveries went quickly and by the time the cart was almost empty, she had to pull over so she could eat the small sandwich and soda she'd packed in the cooler for her lunch. As she sat on the side of the road, people stopped and talked to her as they made their way around the island. There were no posted speed limits and everyone knew everyone else, which made it easier for her to make her deliveries, since people tended to leave their homes unlocked.

Half of her clients left instructions for her to deliver and put away their groceries, which she did without a qualm. But Mrs. Mette was a whole other breed. Even though she should have been her next stop, Missy waited until after she'd delivered the other two deliveries before heading back towards the older woman's house.

Here, on the farthest and most secluded tip of the island, there wasn't a paved road; instead, the sand had been cleared for carts and cars to get through. Most of the homes along this part of the path were accessible by water only. Yet her cart easily made the trek since she'd replaced the smaller tires just last year with larger ones that had high-traction treads. It was a bumpy ride that she couldn't make in bad weather, but she enjoyed it. It was like going four-wheeling or riding in a sand buggy. She loved seeing the white sand kick up behind her as she flew towards the largest house on the island.

Mrs. Mette was in her late sixties and looked like she was at least twenty years older, probably due to the amount of time the woman spent in a bathing suit sitting out by the huge swimming pool in the back of her house.

Her home was far away from anyone else and Missy had it on good authority that Mrs. Mette didn't always bathe with a suit on. She cringed at the thought and took a deep breath, silently praying that today would be one of the woman's more sane days.

She pulled the handcart off the back and piled on the two large boxes of Mrs. Mette's items. When she finally made it through the sand to the small boardwalk and up the stairs, Mrs. Mette was already holding the door open for her.

"I was beginning to wonder if you'd forgotten about me." The older woman smiled at her. Missy noted that she was wearing a long silk cover over her suit today. She was thankful that it appeared to be one of her better days.

"No, just a very busy delivery day." She smiled and stopped the cart in front of the door.

"Oh, good. Well, come on in." She held the door open.

It still got to Missy, seeing the amount of wealth this lone woman had. Even though she'd chosen to seclude herself on an island in the Gulf of Mexico and had no car or other means of transportation that Missy knew of, the woman was wealthy beyond belief.

The furniture alone must have cost more than Missy's little cottage home, which she was so very proud of. Italian tile, marble, stone, and some of the richest, warmest woods she'd ever seen filled the more than six-thousand-square-foot place that was this woman's entire world.

The outside of the home looked nothing like the inside. Outside, the place was plain, boring. It was a fairly square home with a large deck and pool off the back. The metal roof was a bright gold, matching the yellowish tint of the walls. There were lots of windows, and each one had storm shutters in case of high winds.

But inside, the house could have come straight off the pages of *Better Homes and Gardens, Millionaire Edition.* Large stone columns separated the two largest rooms, and high ceilings made the rooms look even bigger. The front room was decorated in all white. Large white sofas with pale blue fluffed pillows sat facing one another on the marbled floors. Thick accent rugs cushioned their footsteps as they walked past the perfect room towards the kitchen area.

There was a large marble dining table, which could easily sit six people, immediately in front of a large island. To say that Mrs. Mette's kitchen was what dreams were made of would have been an understatement.

The first time Missy had seen it, she'd dreamed about it for the rest of that month.

Large, warm wood planks ran along the high ceiling as soon as you passed through the stone archways into the kitchen area. Two large chandeliers hung high over the dining table. Missy just knew that they each cost more than her car.

The kitchen itself was completely white, like the rest of the downstairs. Its high cabinets and stone counter-tops always gleamed. Actually, Missy had never seen anything out of place in the house. Mrs. Mette seemed to not belong in the gleaming cleanliness.

She stopped her cart in front of the bar area and quickly got to work putting each item in its designated spot, noting when she found the woman was low on other items on the checklist she'd created almost six years ago.

"You're running low on wild rice," she said absentmindedly as she continued to put the items away.

"Yes, I had a few guests over the other night." The woman sighed and leaned against the counter, watching Missy's every move.

"Oh?" She smiled at the woman and jotted down to deliver two more boxes the next trip.

"Yes, well." The woman shook her head and glanced out the window, something Missy had never seen her do before. Mrs. Mette had always kept a very keen eye on her movements when she was there, almost like she didn't trust her to not steal anything or, worse, drop something and make a mess.

"Is everything all right?" she asked, turning to

the older woman when she noticed a sad look cross her eyes.

The woman glanced back at her and then blinked a few times. “Yes, of course it is.” She straightened her shoulders and Missy saw that she was back to her old self. She turned back to the task at hand.

“Are you married?” Mrs. Mette asked out of the blue.

For the six and a half years that Missy had been delivering this woman’s groceries, she’d never asked her a personal question. Until now.

“No.” She frowned as she put away the last can of tomato soup. Then she turned towards Mrs. Mette.

“Have you ever been?” The older woman had her arms crossed over her chest and was leaning back on the marble counter-tops.

Missy shook her head, unsure of what had brought on the line of questioning. Sure, she was friendly with most of the customers she delivered for. Most of them knew her life story and she knew theirs. It wasn’t as if she’d been hiding anything from anyone. A deep feeling in her gut made its way to her heart and she felt it skip a beat. Okay, maybe just a few things.

“Why?” She set the empty box back onto her cart and glanced at the older woman again. The woman sighed and glanced out of the window once more.

"It's hard." Her eyes moved towards Missy's. "Living alone. Being alone all the time." She shook her head and Missy thought she saw a tear pool in the corner of her eye before she turned her head to look back out towards the water. "We're not meant for it."

"Mrs. Met—"

"Ruth." The woman turned towards her. "You've been delivering my groceries for how many years?"

Missy blinked. "A little over six."

"And in all that time, you have never once been unkind to me or shown me anything but respect. You should be able to call me by my first name. Ruth."

Missy nodded and smiled. "Ruth, are you sure everything is all right?"

Ruth smiled and nodded. "Your first name is Missy, correct?" Missy nodded. "Missy, do me a favor…"

Missy's heart sank as she thought about making another trip back to the mainland to grab an item Ruth had forgotten.

"Don't let life pass you by without letting someone into your life. Someone who'll love you." She turned her head and looked out the window again. "Someone to be there in the silence of the night and hold you tight."

When Ruth's eyes moved back to hers, Missy nodded. There was a knot deep in her throat, which she tried to swallow the entire trip back to Dog's Landing.

When she walked through the door of the store almost an hour later, she heard Jenny laughing in the back room. Walking towards the sound, she stopped cold when she saw the back of a man's head, leaning over her employee.

"Oh!" she exclaimed and started to turn away. She'd never seen Jenny involved with anyone before, even though she knew the girl had in the past had a few boyfriends.

"Wait." Jenny rushed after her. "It's not like it looked." She giggled. "Roman was just…"

Nothing else Jenny said could get past the loud ringing she heard in her ears.

Roman.

Roman.

She'd just been thinking about her Roman, thanks to the conversation with Ruth.

She blinked a few times when Jenny's fingers dug into her shoulders. Then her hearing returned.

"Are you okay?" Jenny was frowning at her as they stood in the small hallway just outside of the break room.

The knot that had built in her throat from her talk with Ruth had traveled farther south and now sat directly over her heart. Missy's fingers shook. She felt a slight sheen instantly coat her skin as she moved her eyes slowly towards the man who was standing just inside the doorway.

He'd changed. A lot, she thought, just as everything faded to white.

Chapter Two

Roman carried the lax body in his arms and laid her on the small sofa in the break room. Jenny was almost hyperventilating and he had to make her sit down before she passed out from worry.

"It's okay, she's just in shock," he said, rushing over to the sink and grabbing a towel, then splashing cold water on it and making his way back to the petite blonde who had passed out at the sight of him.

Not that he hadn't thought of doing the same, but there was something more than surprise that had crossed his mind.

Looking down at her, he noticed all the changes. Her hair was shorter, cut just above her shoulders. It was still the rich honey blonde that he remembered. Since her eyes were closed, he couldn't see if they were still their warm caramel color.

When he laid the cool cloth over her face, she jumped up and pushed it aside, her eyes going huge as her sexy mouth hung open.

He'd always loved her mouth. Even when he shouldn't have noticed how appealing it was.

"What are you doing here?" she blurted out.

He chuckled. "I work here."

She blinked a few times and he was pleased to see her mouth move silently as she tried to talk. Finally, she swallowed and he watched her control return a bit. "You what?"

He smiled and stood up from his crouched spot in front of her. "I work here. As of a few minutes ago." He glanced over at Jenny, the pretty blonde that had hired him less than ten minutes before.

"No you don't." Marissa stood up, putting her hands on her hips and glaring at him. "I don't want you…"

He took her shoulders and shook her lightly. "Do you really want to do this? Here? Now?" His eyes bore into hers and he felt her stiffen under his hands.

Finally, after she'd glanced towards Jenny and

then back at him, she sighed and he felt her shoulders relax.

"Why?" The word was a whisper as he dropped his hands. After all this time, he still couldn't trust himself to touch her.

"Why am I here?" His eyes moved over to Jenny, who was making a slow retreat out the door. Smart girl, he thought, and then he looked back to Marissa, who shook her head slowly.

"Why do you want to work here?"

His smile was quick as he took a step closer to her. "I have a few questions for you as well."

He watched her breath hitch as she swayed a little. His hands went back up and took her shoulders once more. "Easy," he murmured.

"I…" She blinked a few times as she looked up at him. Her hand went to the side of her head. "I can't…" Her eyes moved to the empty doorway and her face got even whiter than it had when she'd seen him standing there. "I have to go." She jerked her shoulders from his hold and rushed from the room quickly.

It took him a few moments to convince himself that she wasn't bolting for good again. He wanted nothing more than to rush after her. Instead, he sat back down and took several deep breaths to calm his anger and his desires.

"Is everything okay?" Jenny's sweet voice sounded from the doorway. He'd liked the young girl immediately upon meeting her.

"Yeah." He looked up at her and frowned. "Sorry." He shook his head as she walked over and sat down in front of him.

"Are you going to tell me what that was all about?"

He sighed and rested his hands on the table between them. Then he shrugged his shoulders. Where should he begin? Was it his place? Looking over, he frowned and shook his head.

"I think that's best for Marissa to tell."

Jenny's eyebrows shot up when he used her full name. He sighed and shook his head, remembering that she'd called her Missy instead. A nick-name he'd always used for her.

"I know everything there is to know about Marissa." She said the name slowly. "I've known her for almost seven years. She's never once in all that time mentioned you." She crossed her arms over her chest and glared at him.

He rolled his shoulders and stood up as he glanced out the large window and watched a boat full of teenagers, along with two older men, dock. "Looks like that's my first job." He nodded towards the window and the loud noises coming from the crowd of people on the docks, hoping the girl would take the change in discussion.

"Roman." Jenny stood and reached for his arm before he could leave. "I stand behind my decision to hire you, but if I think for one minute that you're bad for Missy, I won't hesitate to fire you on the spot."

He smiled quickly and nodded. "Gotcha." He liked her even more for saying so.

Then he walked out the back door to get trained for his new job, knowing he would do whatever it took to stick as close to Marissa—Missy—as possible.

***

Missy slammed the door behind her and locked it. Then, for good measure, she leaned against it and braced herself. She'd run too fast to glance over her shoulder to see if he was following her. She'd always been able to outrun Roman.

When everything remained quiet, she chanced a peek out the window and sighed when the street in front of her home was empty. Rushing to the back door, she opened her key drawer and pulled out the keys. She jumped behind the wheel of her car, her eyes darting everywhere as she pulled slowly out of the garage behind her house.

She couldn't hear anything over the roar of the V8 engine in her classic '65 Ford Falcon. She'd put less than two thousand miles on the baby since she'd sprung for it a few years back, but when she peeled out of her driveway this time, she planned on putting a whole lot more miles on it.

As she drove, even the car mocked her. She'd

only bought the classic because Roman had always talked about getting his hands on the exact car one day. She couldn't remember how many times he'd mentioned that he'd dreamed of the day when he could afford one, how he'd spend his time and money fixing it up.

Fighting the urge to bang her head against the steering wheel, she gripped it tighter. It had been an impulse buy. She'd seen it sitting just down the street from her shop and had instantly felt like she knew the car. Maybe it was her subconscious telling her that she could be close to him.

For years, she'd fought the urge to go back and see her family, to be a part of their lives again. Several times in the past, she'd chanced a day trip to Spring Haven. But each time she'd come back, empty hearted and full of fear that she'd been seen.

By the time she finally pulled in front of the school, she had somewhat talked herself out of leaving, like last time. She wasn't going to make the same mistake she'd made when she was young and stupid. After all, this time was different. This time he was in her town. Her home. Her business. After all, who was he to waltz in and turn her life upside down?

It wasn't like he scared her. No, just the opposite. After all, it wasn't fear that had shot through her veins when he'd touched her.

She tried not to think of how her body had responded to his touch. Or what it meant to her to see him again.

She took a few moments to calm herself down before walking into the front office. Even though it was summer, she knew that Reagan would be totally engrossed in his studies. When he'd begged her to enroll him in the summer reading program, she'd hesitated. In the end, it had been a blessing, since he didn't have to spend all of his summer stuck down at the store with her.

When she walked towards the doorway of the small room, filled only with three kids and Mrs. Miller, the principal of the school, she sighed as she leaned her head against the glass in the door and watched her son.

His dark head was down as he read from a book. She knew his dark eyes would take in every detail of the words he was silently reading. Even though he had already read the required summer class reading, he was totally engrossed in what he was doing. He always read when he was bored with his regular homework during the school year, which meant he was ahead in all of his classes. He'd always been ahead of his classmates, but this summer program was pushing him even farther ahead. She'd thought about moving him up a grade, but so far, she'd held off making that decision.

Mrs. Miller's eyes moved to the doorway and met hers. Her eyebrows shot up in question. Missy had never visited during the summer before.

“Is there a problem?” she asked after opening the door for her.

“N…no.” She shook her head and took a breath. “I…” She sighed. “I just…”

“Mom?” Reagan rushed over to her and hugged her. “We’re reading *Holes* again.” His entire face lit up. “I’m at the part—”

“Reagan, maybe your mother would like to come in and sit with you for a while?” Mrs. Miller smiled and opened the door a crack.

Missy felt her eyes tear up, so she nodded quickly and let her son lead her into the room.

“Can I take her to the reading corner?” Reagan asked eagerly. The reading corner was an old claw tub filled with over-sized pillows.

Mrs. Miller smiled and nodded, and Reagan continued to pull her towards the back of the classroom.

She settled in the old tub with her son on her lap, his head resting on her shoulder, and listened to him read her one of his favorite books. Only then did everything become crystal clear. Everything she’d done in the last eight years had been for one reason. Their son.

***

It was late afternoon, just before sunset, when Roman finally saw Marissa again. He’d gone out on two runs with the older gentlemen showing him all of the ropes. Since he was already up to speed on how to drive the boat, he spent most of his energy learning how to safely secure the parasailers and deal with the gear properly.

By the end of the day, he knew all there was to know about parasailing and keeping customers safe. When he walked into the store with Bob and John around closing time, Missy was standing behind the counter instead of Jenny.

She had glanced up with a smile on her face until her eyes moved over him, then her smile faltered and fell away quickly.

"How was it?" she asked, keeping her eyes on the older gentlemen.

John walked over and leaned on the counter next to her. "You know how it goes." He smiled. "You win some, you lose some."

She laughed and slapped him on the shoulder playfully. John was a bear of an old man at six foot three and two hundred fifty pounds, unlike his partner in crime, Bob, who stood only five foot five and probably weighed as much as a teenage cheerleader.

The two of them were a very likable duo who'd peppered him with a million questions once he'd climbed aboard the boat and informed them he was a new hire.

One of the first questions from Frank had been, "Aren't you a little old to have a job like this?" He's just raised his eyebrows and glanced slowly at the two of them, and they had laughed and slapped him on the back. That hadn't stopped the barrage of questions, most of them tailored around his career choices and if he was single.

"This new guy of yours…"—Bob slapped him on the back as he walked by to hang the boat keys on a hook behind the counter—"sure has a way with the ladies." Bob winked at him behind Marissa's back.

Marissa started coughing and turned beet red. "He's…" She cleared her throat. "He's not mine." She frowned. "I mean." Her eyes traveled everywhere but near him. "Jenny hired him."

He chuckled and leaned against the counter. "Yeah, but knowing our history…" He smiled when he saw her eyes heat and finally zero in on his.

"Oh!" John chuckled. "You two have a history?"

Bob walked over and leaned against the counter, making a point to nudge Marissa.

"So, tell us all."

She closed her eyes, and he heard a soft growl coming from her throat. He smiled. "Sure, why don't you tell them all about it."

Her eyes flew open and he saw her caramel eyes heat further. He knew he was pushing her, but after all she'd put his family—him—through, she deserved it. At least a little.

"He's..." She blinked and he heard a slight chuckle. "It's complicated." He smiled and leaned closer to her and nodded.

Good, he thought. That's exactly how he felt about her. He leaned against the counter until the older men and customers had left. He liked watching the way she dealt with people. He especially liked watching her as she moved around the small space behind the counter as she closed out for the evening. Even with him crowding her, she handled herself well. She'd always been light on her feet and moved almost like a dancer.

"Will you please go wait in the back," she finally growled out. He smiled back at her and shook his head no.

"What?" She turned around and crossed her arms over her chest. "Do you think I'm going to run away?"

His eyebrows shot up. "Again?" He thought about it, looked around, and slowly shook his head no. "Not this time." It came out more as a warning than an answer.

She blinked and tried to back up a step, only to have his hands reach out and take her by the shoulder. "Don't," he said softly. He hated seeing the fear that had jumped into her eyes.

She shook her head and closed her eyes. "What do you expect? After all this time, you show up here. Like this." Her eyes met his.

"It should have never had to come to this." His voice was soft.

"You knew." She backed up a step and he let his hands drop next to him. "You knew why I had to leave."

He shook his head, his eyes still glued to hers. "No. I didn't. No one knew." He'd always wondered if it had something to do with him. With their relationship, but other than that, he was just as clueless as the rest of the family. Shortly before she'd disappeared, she'd shocked him by going out on a date with his buddy Tommy. Which had done nothing but piss him off. They'd fought about it a few days before she'd gone, but he'd always believed that they'd worked it out and that she'd decided to end the short-lived relationship with Tommy.

"I saw you." She broke into his thoughts, her face turned red.

"When?"

"That night." Her chin dropped a little.

He frowned. "The night you left?"

She swallowed and nodded slowly.

"Marissa, I don't know what you're talking about. I didn't see you the night you left. No one did. All we had was the note you'd written Cassey."

Upon hearing their sister's name, her eyes filled with tears and she looked down at her hands nervously.

"But..." She blinked and he watched the tears stream down her face. "I saw you in your room."

He slowly shook his head, not really trusting his voice.

"I saw you..." Her eyes flew up to his and she almost shouted. "With Susan Shaffer."

Chapter Three

Missy watched him blink a few times as he took a step back. Then he started to laugh. Hard. He laughed until she felt like walking over to him and punching him as hard as she could.

When he looked up again, she was staring at him like he'd gone mad.

He walked over to her and took her shoulders with his hands then pulled her close. "You saw Marcus with Susan."

"No," she ground out. "I saw you and Susan… on your bed. Together." She still remembered the hurt the scene had caused her. The years of pain that had caused her to never allow herself to get close to anyone since.

She'd always chalked it up to him being made about the one date she'd gone on with one of his friends. To be honest, she couldn't even remember the boys name. She'd been foolish enough to think that she needed to try seeing other guys to gauge if she would ever feel different about Roman. Since she knew there was no way they could ever be together. Not when they were both Graytons.

"You saw Marcus and Susan on my bed. Believe me. I must have walked in a few minutes after you did. I spent a few minutes cussing them out for defiling my space."

When he smiled this time, she felt her heart skip then sink into her stomach when his words finally penetrated her mind. "But…" Her chin fell. "You…" Her head shook from side to side as the realization hit her.

He closed his eyes and took a few deep breaths. "All this time…"

She straightened her shoulders and then pushed him away. It didn't matter. It would have never worked. She didn't belong in Spring Haven, just like he didn't belong in Carrabelle.

"It doesn't matter anyway. It never would have worked out." She slammed open the cash register and stuffed all the cash into the bank bag, and then bent over to shove it all in the safe.

"Why?" The simple question hung in the air.

She turned quickly towards him and frowned. "Because we're..." She couldn't say it. The word *related* was like a curse to her, even after all this time.

"Adopted?" He smiled. "There's no blood between us." He crossed his arms over his chest.

She felt all the blood drain from her face and swayed a little. Oh, how untrue that statement was.

"Easy." He frowned and started walking towards her. She held up her hand quickly and leaned against the counter.

"No, don't." She took a few breaths to clear her head.

He nodded and then dropped his hands by his sides. "Missy." Hearing him use his nickname for her sent a wave of lust straight to her bones. "We were adopted into a wonderful family. Raised as brother and sister, but we both know..." He took a step towards her again, slowly. "We never felt that way about one another." Her eyes met his. "Never."

"Roman." It came out as a whisper. "I..." She shook her head, not sure what to say.

"Why?" The word this time was almost an accusation.

"Why, what?" She felt her shoulders hunch.

"Why did you stay away?" His voice seemed distant. Angry. She knew she deserved every ounce of his anger. Especially after finding out it hadn't been him that night, all those years ago.

She shook her head and rolled her neck, trying to release all the negative energy. "I don't know. I guess I was hurt. Angry." She looked at him. "Scared."

"Of what was between us?" He'd moved closer to her.

She nodded slightly. When he moved to touch her, she backed up and held her hands between them. "No." The simple word made him stop. "I can't have you touching me."

"Why?" He frowned, but nodded. "Why not come back?"

She felt almost hysterical. "Why?" She repeated the word, letting it roll off her tongue. "So many different reasons." She jerked her arms around, waving them around like a mad person. "This place, my place. My house, my car. My life." She turned towards him. "I have a home here. I've made something from nothing. All by myself."

He nodded. "I'm not asking you to give it all up. Just come back. Visit."

She sighed and then rubbed the side of her head with her fingers. It was starting to pound and she wanted nothing more than to escape again. The guilt was too much. She knew that. All those years she'd thought about returning to Spring Haven. All those day's she'd desperately wished to see her sister and other brothers again.

"Missy, there's nothing stopping you," he whispered.

"Yes." She nodded. "Everything is stopping me. I have to go." She glanced at the clock. "I'll tell Jenny you've left. I'm sure she'll be able to find someone—"

"No."

"What?" She frowned and glanced at him.

"I'm not leaving unless you come with me." He crossed his arms over his chest, a move she remembered too well.

She laughed. "Then you'd better settle in." She walked over to the door with her purse and keys in hand, waiting for him to follow her. She flipped off the lights as he walked out of the store and locked the door with her key.

"I plan on it," he said behind her. When she turned around, he shocked her by taking her into his arms and laying his lips quickly over hers.

There was anger, fear, and desperation behind the move, and she felt every ounce of emotion that crossed between them until, finally, she settled on the pure enjoyment of the moment. His mouth slanted over hers, sending heat all the way to her toes. She'd forgotten what it felt like. Being held, kissed, touched.

When he slowly pulled away, she was sure he would be able to see her body vibrating. Instead of smiling at her weakness, like he used to so many years ago, he frowned and watched her closely, waiting for her to respond.

When she could finally think again, she asked, "Where are you staying?" She tried to get herself under control as he answered..

"The motel a few blocks away." He nodded down the street. He looked so calm, like the kiss hadn't affected him as much as it had her. Hurt and anger started to spread throughout her again.

She laughed harshly. "Which one?"

He shrugged his shoulders. "The blue one."

If he could act so calm, then she should be able to shake that kiss off as quickly as he had.

"First customers arrive at seven." She turned and started walking down the stairs, feeling proud of herself for holding it together.

"Wait." He rushed after her. "Why don't I walk you home?"

She shook her head, not wanting to look at him.. "I drove." She motioned to her car and watched his eyebrows shoot up.

He walked over and ran a finger over the paint. "This…is yours?"

She smiled, feeling proud that at least now he was showing jealousy. Then she crossed her arms over her chest and frowned at him as he held his hands out for the keys. She frowned and just looked at him.

"Oh, come on!" He smiled, showing off a dimple near his mouth that she remembered too well. "You know that's my dream car. How could you do this to me and not let me drive her?"

She chuckled. "Her?" She shook her head and then smiled. "You're a grown man now." She felt her face heat when she realized just how grown he was and how that kiss had started something inside her. "Get used to disappointments." She walked around him, jumped behind the wheel, and turned the key. Just for kicks, she revved the engine a little before putting it in reverse.

She glanced at him and watched his eyes almost water as she peeled out of the parking spot.

***

Roman watched his dream car and woman disappear and felt his heart jump with excitement.

Not until her brake lights disappeared did he feel like he finally had his heart back under control. He stood in the balmy night, letting the bugs swarm around him as he stood under the parking light, replaying everything that had just happened.

What he wanted to do was jump in his car, which was parked two blocks away, and follow her to make sure she wasn't going to pack up and leave once more.

Deciding she had too much at stake this time, he turned towards his hotel and slowly walked the few blocks, trying to calm himself down. Why was she being so secretive? Why wouldn't she come home? What was keeping her away from the family that loved her?

He stopped off at the small family-owned restaurant next to his hotel and grabbed a burger. The place was packed with at least a dozen people who were crammed into a place built for only thirty. He sat along the old-time bar and wolfed down his burger and fries, and then he topped it off with a milk shake, since the family next to him was enjoying them and they looked delicious. He wasn't disappointed.

When he'd been young, there had been a place like this in Surf Breeze on the boardwalk. Now it was a yoga place. Shaking his head, he watched the families interact. He loved small towns. The feeling that everyone knew everyone else, the welcoming sense you got as you walked through a door and someone called out your name. Even if you were in a hurry to get dinner to go, you always had time to stop and talk to someone you knew.

He couldn't stop the memories coming as he watched the scene. Even though his family had been duct taped together, it had held strong. Until Marissa had shattered it when she'd left all those years ago.

When he finally strolled into his hotel room, he realized he was exhausted from the long day in the sun.

His dream started like they always did when he dreamed about Marissa—on the day he met her.

***

"Give it back!" Cole said over and over again as he jumped, trying to get the small book from Roman's hands, which were stretched as high as he could get them above his head. The recent discovery that he had grown a few inches taller than Cole had filled him with delight. And in the last few weeks, he'd done everything he could to annoy his younger brother, whom he'd just met for the first time a little under a year ago.

Even though the makeshift family wasn't related by blood, that didn't stop any of them from acting like it. The three boys got along better than most of the other siblings in their school. He supposed it had to do with who they lived with.

The Graytons were gold. Not only did Mark, their old man, and Elizabeth, their new mother, show them nothing but patience and kindness, but Julie—Mark and Elizabeth's daughter—was like a second mother to them all. Julie was the one who really spent most of her time with Roman.

He wasn't sure why she treated him differently than the others. But he'd needed that attention when he'd first arrived.

His body had been badly damaged. He'd had a cast on and more cuts and bruises than he'd ever had before.

"Julie!" Cole stopped jumping and crossed his arms over his small chest. Then he jerked his head to the side to push his wild mass of hair away from his eyes. The kid's blonde hair was longer than Julie's at this point.

"Get a haircut," Roman groaned as he handed over the book and stuck out his tongue.

Cole never could play fair. He knew that Roman's weakness was seeing the disappointment in Julie's eyes as she scolded him. Just the fear of it always caused him to cave.

"Go climb a tree," Cole shot back and raced off.

Just then they heard a car drive up. When he rushed to the windows that overlooked the front yard, he was happily surprised to see Lilly's silver sedan bump up the driveway.

"It's Lilly!" he shouted out to everyone in the house as he raced down the stairs, wanting to be the first one out the door to greet their new sister.

It was all everyone had been talking about for the last three days, ever since Elizabeth had gotten the call from Lilly, their guardian angel. Or so she liked to be called because she worked for the state and helped find lost kids new homes.

She'd saved his butt, along with Marcus's and Cole's. The three boys owed the woman more than they could ever repay.

When he reached the front porch, his breath

caught in his throat and he felt a stabbing pain shoot straight to his gut.

There, standing before him, was another angel, one his size, dressed in a soft pink dress with white flowers and a pink bow tied around her waist. Her yellow hair flowed around her shoulders, going almost all the way down to her knees. It looked softer than he ever knew was possible.

"Oh, there's one now. Roman, this is your new sister, Marissa."

He blinked a few times, instantly hating the word sister.

Her caramel eyes met his, then her chin dropped along as she looked at his feet. He'd been in such a hurry to be the first one out the door that he'd forgotten to put on his shoes. Normally that wouldn't have mattered, but since they'd spent the entire morning getting dressed up in their church clothes to meet their new sister, he supposed he looked funny in a suit with no shoes.

Glancing down, he wiggled his toes and frowned. "I forgot my shoes," he said, looking back up at Lilly, who only laughed.

"I'm sure you'll find them around somewhere. Is anyone else home?"

He nodded quickly, then stood aside and opened the front porch door. "They're probably in the kitchen. We've made a big dinner for her." He nodded and noticed that Marissa's eyes were still glued to his feet.

"Well, I'll just go on back. Roman, why don't you show Marissa around." Lilly said.

"Sure," he said, not really paying attention to Lilly as she disappeared down the hallway.

"You want to look around?" he asked, shoving his hands into his pockets.

She slowly shook her head from side to side, her eyes still fixed on the floor.

"You can talk, can't you?" he asked after a minute.

She nodded her head.

"Well," he sighed and glanced around. "This is the front porch. We hang out here a lot ever since Marcus and I rebuilt it." His chest puffed out a little when the pride hit him. He still couldn't believe how great it had turned out.

He watched her eyes move up and over the large space. Then she blinked and he watched in horror as a tear escaped.

"Hey." He took a step back. "Don't do that." He frowned as another one fell onto the new flooring.

She shook her eyes and started wiping the tears that were flooding out now.

"Did someone hit you?" he asked, moving closer.

She glanced at him and shook her head no.

"Well, then, count yourself lucky." He was so close to her now, he could smell the slight hint of sweet flowers on her. "You sure do smell good," he mumbled, not realizing he'd said it out loud.

Her eyes met his and he watched her blink away the tears as she watched him.

"I..." She closed her eyes. "I was getting married."

He blinked a few times and then chuckled, thinking she was making a funny joke.

She frowned and her eyes moved back to the floor.

"That's a funny one." He moved to tap her on the shoulder, only to have her pull away quickly. "Hey." He frowned. "We don't hit here." He moved closer to her and tilted his head as he watched her. "You're serious?" His voice squeaked. "Really?"

She glanced up at him, tears falling again. Then she bolted.

For a girl, she sure could run fast. They were almost all the way to the lake before he caught up with her. He grabbed her arm and yanked her to a stop. "Easy!" he said, holding her still, only to have her shiny black shoes rise up and kick him square in the shins, shins that had seen many bruises in the past.

"Ouch!" He hopped up and down on his good leg while still holding her. "Why'd you go and do that?"

"You..." She cried out. "You don't know anything. You're just a stupid boy!" Her face was almost beet red as more tears poured from her eyes.

"Well, sure I am. And you're a stupid girl." He smiled and nodded his head, feeling accomplished.

She glared back at him. "Let go of me!" she screamed in his face. He dropped his hands.

"Don't kick me." He took a step back when she made a move. She just glared back at him.

"I don't like boys. I never want to be around another one for as long as I live." She crossed her arms over her chest.

He laughed. "Well, then you're going to have a very boring life. Boys are a lot of fun. Besides, you've got three brothers now." He leaned closer and whispered. "You can't avoid us."

Chapter Four

Roman's alarm woke him from the dream, so he rolled out of bed, wishing he'd had a few more hours of sleep.

Pulling on a clean pair of swim trunks and a tank top, he slipped into his shoes as he made his way out the door. He could get used to the easy life. Not that he didn't love wearing his normal attire of suits and ties. But, underneath it all, he had always loved the ease of beach shorts and flip-flops.

When he walked up to the store, he frowned when he didn't spot Missy's red beauty in the parking lot.

The bell chimed when he walked in and he smiled and sighed with relief when she called from the back room, “Be there in a minute.”

Making his way to the back, he was rewarded when he walked into the supply room and bumped solidly into the back of her. She’d climbed up a small stepladder and had both of her arms over her head, holding a large box. It didn’t look heavy, just awkward.

Instantly, his hands reached out and steadied her before she fell from the perch. Her hips were smaller than he remembered and he had a nice view of her backside, which he didn’t want to give up just yet. Holding her still, he felt her stiffen when his fingers tightened on her hips.

“I’m fine,” she said without turning around. “You can let go of me now.”

“Can’t.” It came out as a whisper and he closed his eyes for just one moment. When he felt her move in his arms, his eyes opened and he watched her set the box down on the shelf. His fingers tightened for just a moment before he released her so she could turn around.

“What are you doing here?” she asked, looking down at him.

“I’m here for you.” His voice had fled and he sounded like he’d just run a marathon. His breathing was uneven and his chest rose and fell quickly as he tried to keep in check.

She shook her head from side to side slowly. "I… I can't do this." She moved to take a step away from him. His hands went automatically to her hips again, keeping her steady on the small ladder.

"Easy," he frowned.

"Roman," she started to say just as the bell chimed. She blinked a few times and then pulled away and walked out of the small supply room without saying anything more.

Gripping the shelves, his knuckles turned white as he prayed that he'd be able to convince her.

He'd dreamed of a million ways to talk her into returning home. To his family. To him. But every time she was around him, none of them came to mind.

Sighing, he turned and walked out of the small room to walk in on Missy hugging a large, very tan, very muscular man. He felt every muscle in his body tense with jealousy.

When he cleared his throat, Missy pulled away from the man, her smile still in place as her eyes met his.

He'd never once thought there was a possibility that she had a lover. He'd learned from his sources that she was unmarried, but they hadn't been able to find out anything more. The fact that it had taken a private detective almost two years to find her had baffled him. Especially considering she was less than a hundred miles away, still going by Marissa, and he'd given the man a few dozen pictures of her. She had changed her last name from Grayton to Wright, which hadn't been even her real mother's name.

As he watched, she reached up on her toes and kissed the man on his cheek. "I'll see you later tonight." She squeezed his shoulder. The man glanced at him with a stern look in his eyes, then back at Missy.

"Is everything okay?" he asked.

Missy didn't even glance his way before answering. "It's fine. I was just showing our newest employee the supplies." She walked behind the counter, dismissing them both.

"New around here, eh?" the man said, taking a few steps towards him. "I'm Clay. I'm one of the ferry captains."

He felt some of the jealousy shift. "Roman." He shook the man's hand when he offered it. "So far I've been on parasailing."

Clay nodded. "Jenny mentioned that the two of you knew each other." He nodded to where Missy was busy behind the counter near the back of the store.

He nodded slowly. "Grew up together." He crossed his arms over his chest.

"You'd better get going. I know Julie will be waiting for you," she called from behind the counter.

He watched Clay turn pale and then nod his head and rush out.

Roman walked over to where Missy was putting all of the cash back into the register.

"What was that about?" he asked, trying to keep his voice level.

She glanced up at him, her eyebrows squished together in question.

"Clay was just coming in to tell me that he needed next month off."

"Oh?" he asked, leaning against the counter, trying to look casual. What he really wanted to do was ask her why she was hugging her employee.

She nodded her head, not even looking up at him this time.

"So, sounds like you'll be needing someone to help out with the ferry." He waited as she sighed and closed her eyes. When she rolled her shoulders, he watched the movement and appreciated the view. She was wearing a black tank top and tan shorts that fit her just right. He wished he could get his hands on her again.

"I hadn't thought that far ahead yet." She turned and glanced at a sheet of paper hanging behind the counter. "Marv is supposed to be on for the next few days."

"Maybe I can ride with him. From the looks of

it, John and Bob have things under control with the parasailing."

She looked over at him and thought about it for a while. "Why?"

He smiled. "Why, what?"

She crossed her arms over her chest. "Are you going to…" Just then the bell chimed again and she groaned with frustration. "Later," she warned. "Do whatever you want. If I remember correctly, you will anyway."

He chuckled as he turned and walked out. They knew each other too well to pretend. Even though they'd been apart almost eight years, he still knew her better than anyone else did.

He stood on the dock, waiting for the ferry to come back from its first run of the day. He'd told Bob and John that he was training with Marv today. The two men had smiled and slapped him on his back.

"Couldn't cut it, huh?"

He'd chuckled. "Well, I just figured that you two had everything under control. Besides, Cole's supposed to be out for a month."

"Oh?" They both looked at each other. "Julie must have had the baby."

He'd been relieved to find out that Cole was married and a new father, which had explained the hug. Still, he spent a few minutes probing the older guys into telling him that Missy was not seeing anyone.

"Actually, come to think of it, she hasn't mentioned dating, ever," Bob had said.

"You know," John said and scratched his chin, "I don't think that girl's been out on a date for years." They both shook their heads and then turned as a group of people lined up to get on the boat.

It was almost half an hour later when Missy walked to the end of the dock, dragging behind her a cart.

"What's all that?" He motioned to the cart full of boxes.

"Deliveries," she'd said and sat next to him.

"For?" He waited patiently.

"Customers." She waved his next question aside. "It's groceries for customers on Dog Island," she finally said. "Now, are you going to tell me what you're doing here?"

Their knees were almost touching. He leaned closer and enjoyed watching her eyes heat when skin touched skin.

"I told you. I'm here for you."

She turned to him, scooting her knee away.

"I'm not going to go back. I couldn't…" She turned and watched the ferry making its way towards them.

"What?" he asked, putting his arm around her.

She sighed and glanced at him. "I couldn't face them. Not after everything." She turned her face into the wind and sun.

"Missy," he said, playing with her hair like he used to. It was still soft and smelled like strawberries like it always had. "No matter what you did in the past"—he used his finger to pull her chin until she looked at him—"we forgive you. We're your family. We love you."

***

Roman's words played over in her head as she sat back and watched Marv teach him everything he would need to know about running the ferry.

She wanted to believe him and wished more than anything that her family could understand why she'd had to leave. Why she couldn't go back.

When her eyes grew damp thinking about it, she stood up and walked outside and leaned against the railing, watching the crystal teal water below her. There was just too much at stake now. She wasn't willing to give up her life. Her career. Even more important, Reagan.

At just the thought of her family finding out her secret, she shivered in the warm air, so she wrapped her arms around herself and leaned against the railing.

No, she wouldn't be going back. She needed to work on a plan to get Roman to leave.

When the ferry docked, Roman helped her unload her cart. Even though there were only two deliveries for the day, she still had four large boxes to lug around. She knew she'd be done in time to catch the next ferry ride home but thought about taking some time to enjoy a walk along the beach first.

Roman showing up had changed so much in her life, she still hadn't had time to think through all the possibilities.

Reagan had been too full of energy last night for her to have a moment to herself. Dinnertime ran into bath time, which of course ran into her reading him a story before bed. Then she'd been too tired to even relax in a hot bath, which she had fantasized about all day.

Her first delivery was to the newest members of Dog Island. The Chen's were newlyweds, direct from San Diego. They were one of the cutest couples Missy had ever had the privilege to meet.

Huan Chen was a local dentist and in his mid-thirties. His wife, Sue, had just graduated and worked out of the home with online legal advice sites.

Sue was one of the nicest clients Missy had ever had. The woman went out of her way to help her unload their groceries and always chatted with her.

By the time she made her other delivery, she was in a better mood, thanks to Sue. She took her time driving to one of her favorite spots on the island where there weren't many homes. She liked the seclusion and the quiet.

Pulling off her shoes, she walked for a few minutes and then found a soft spot in the white sugar sand to sit down. Tucking her knees up to her chest, she sat and watched the crystal-clear teal water lap on the shore and thought about Roman.

So much had changed since she'd seen him last. Even though he looked pretty much the same, so much had changed about him. His hair for one. She held in a giggle, then glanced around and, realizing she was truly alone, let it out anyway.

She'd never seen it as long as it was now. He looked like a beach bum, more like Cole than the Roman she'd known. Roman had always been neat and tidy. Perfect.

She sighed and rested her head against her knees. Perfect. She thought about that word. So many years ago, she'd thought that's exactly what he was. Perfect.

Hadn't that been the reason she'd fallen for him right away? And also the reason she'd left in such haste.

She'd been a mess when she'd arrived at the Grayton's, not knowing who to trust or even if she could trust herself.

Even with all of her current indecision, she was far better off now than she'd been as a child.

Brainwashing was a hard thing to get over. Especially if it was done by people you loved and trusted and it started before you could walk.

Shaking her head clear of the horror that was her life growing up in a polygamous sect, she moved back to thoughts of Roman. How he'd been the one to help her grow out of her fear of the opposite sex.

He'd earned her trust, her friendship, then her love, all within the first year of knowing him.

Then she'd betrayed him and left him and her family in the dark as she ran. Looking back at her life, she realized that all the reasons she'd piled up didn't really account for the hurt she'd caused them.

She cared too much about them. When she'd heard that Cole had been in an accident, she'd rushed to the hospital to check up on him, afraid that she'd be seen, but more afraid that her brother had been seriously injured.

Then there had been Cassey's wedding. Sighing, she glanced up and looked out over the water. She'd cried herself to sleep that night. It had been so hard, standing along the boardwalk, almost two hundred yards away, watching her sister get married. Several times, she'd talked herself into running across the sand and rushing up to take her sister in a hug.

But, in the end, she'd spotted Roman standing

next to her other brothers and had backed away slowly. She just couldn't imagine telling him everything. Not then and not now.

She knew it was inevitable. Everything in life moved in a big circle. She'd tried to prepare herself for the day she would have to tell Roman about Reagan.

Falling back onto the sand, she looked up at the cloud-free sky and moaned. "Why did it have to happen so fast?"

Chapter Five

Being a captain of a ferry was a lot more fun than he'd ever imagined. First of all, you got to greet everyone who boarded and exited your vessel. Second, you got to steer a bad-ass large boat with a lot of power. Third, you got to say anything you wanted over the loudspeakers and you had a captive audience.

Of course, by the third trip, he'd run out of jokes and material, but that didn't matter to the passengers; they laughed and clapped along anyway.

Marv had shown him all that he could by the

end of the first run. He'd promised to show him about the engines and mechanics after their last run of the day, which ended around seven thirty in the evenings.

"We don't run after dark. There are a few ferries farther down that run after sunset, but not us." The older man smiled at him as he waved to a few people leaving the docks. "We won't run during a storm either. Only before and after we've gotten the all clear."

"Why's that?" he asked, leaning against the railing of the dock.

"Too many chances. Missy's old man had a crew that took chances." He shook his head. "Lost three good men in one day."

He stood up, dropping his arms to his sides. "Missy's old…" He shook his head. "Her father?"

Marv glanced at him. "I thought you said you grew up with her?"

"I did…" He fought the urge to tell the man everything. "I know for a fact that Missy was adopted at the age of eight."

Marv smiled and nodded. "Then she found Doug shortly after her eighteenth birthday. Right before she had Reagan."

"Reagan?" His head was starting to spin.

"Whoa, are you okay? You're not seasick or something, are you?"

"Marv, you and I need to have a talk. Now." He gripped the man's arm and pulled him back towards the ferry.

Thirty minutes later, the ferry was pulling back up to the island docks. When he saw Missy standing at the docks next to a few customers, he turned to Marv.

"I'm taking a break. You can pick us up on the next run."

Marv nodded and then slapped him on the back. "Be patient with her."

He answered. "You've no idea how patient I've already been."

As he exited the boat, her eyes settled on him. She looked relaxed. Like she'd gotten a little more sun that day. Her blonde hair was flying around her face and she started to smile when she saw him. When her eyes met his, however, the smile fell away.

"What?" she asked when he walked up to her without saying a word and took her arm. "What's wrong?" She glanced back at the ferry, then at him. "Did Marv…"

"Not here," he growled, pulling her with him until he stood in front of the cart. "This is yours?" he asked. When she nodded, he moved aside to allow her to climb aboard. "I'll drive." He waited until she scooted over on the seat.

"Roman, you don't…"

"Not yet." He looked at her, trying to swallow his hurt, pain, and anger until he was better under control. When the cart kicked up dust behind them, he smiled. The last thing he'd wanted was to be putting along in a golf cart when there was so much bubbling up inside him. Right now, he needed the speed.

They rode along in silence. She propped her feet up on the dash like she was along for a slow Sunday drive, so he gunned it again until the pavement ended. Then he sped through the sand until they were finally out of land. Here, there were only a few houses scattered few and far between. He drove until he found a patch of beach that was far away from anything else. When the cart stopped, she turned to him on the seat and raised her eyebrows.

"Are you going to tell me what this is all about?"

He rolled his shoulders before turning to her and taking her hand in his. Then he tugged until she followed him to the edge of the water.

"Tell me it's not true." He didn't recognize his own voice.

"Wh… what?" He watched her swallow.

Instead of answering, he just looked at her.

"Roman?" She shook her head. "Marv had no right…"

He let out a low growl, causing her to stop.

"Is it true?" he asked again.

She sighed and crossed her arms over her chest, a move he knew all too well. There was nothing more he would get from her, not if he continued to go at it from this angle.

Years of loneliness, hurt, and anger boiled inside of him along with newer emotions of betrayal, of being lied to, raped of something he'd desired beyond anything else. Everything mixed together caused him to move towards her in a quick motion.

Before he knew it, she was in his arms, her lips crushed under his as he took what he'd wanted for what seemed like forever.

Her nails dug into his skin just below his ribs. She didn't even try to push him away. Instead she met him beat for beat, moan for moan as he fueled his desires with the taste, the feel of her next to him.

When her knees went lax, he followed her to the soft sand, covering her body with his, pushing her farther into the beach.

Not until he felt her heart kick against his chest, her breathing labored so much that she was gulping for oxygen, did he finally push away from her.

He sat next to her and shoved his fingers through his hair, almost yanking it all out. "Why?" It came out as a whisper.

She took her time sitting up, tucking her knees close to her chest and wrapping her arms around them.

"I was afraid."

He turned quickly to her. "Of me?"

She shook her head without looking at him.

"Then what?" he croaked.

"My family." She bit her bottom lip.

The burst of laughter escaped him. "We would have…"

"No, not the Graytons." She turned to him finally. "The Smiths."

He tilted his head in question. "You don't have a family outside of…"

She sighed and rolled her head back, looking directly above her. "Roman," she finally said, turning to him again. "Do you remember what I said the day we met?"

He smiled. "You hated boys."

She nodded. "And?" When he didn't answer, she continued. "I said it was my wedding day."

He chuckled. "Yeah, still haven't gotten…" His voice died in the breeze when realization hit him. His shoulders slumped and he felt his insides shake with something else—fear and anger mixed together.

His fingers took her shoulders and pulled her

closer. "You were serious?"

She nodded and he watched a tear roll down her cheek.

"What has that got to do with why you left me?"

She closed her eyes and he could tell she was trying to get her emotions under control.

"Everything." She shook her head, which sent her hair flying around her damp face.

He thought about it for a moment and realized he had yet to hear one thing from her.

"Is the boy mine?" he asked quietly.

***

How could she tell him so much without exposing everything. Before answering, she turned to look off at the surf. The waves were stronger here, at the end of the island. Angrier, like Roman was, sitting next to her.

"Yes." She turned to him, watching his emotions. She expected anger, but not his tears. When he closed his eyes, several rolled down his face, breaking her heart in two.

"I didn't know I was pregnant with I left." She reached for him, only to have him yank away and stand up. When he walked several feet into the surf, she followed. "You have to believe me."

After a moment, he turned to her, looking deep

into her eyes. "Why didn't you come back? After you found out?"

She dropped her arms. "My family…" When his eyes heated, she corrected her statement. "The Smith's found me."

"What has that got to do with us?" His voice vibrated with anger.

"The Smith's run the Council of Friends." She waited until realization dawned in his eyes.

"The cult?" he asked.

When she nodded, his hands went to her shoulders.

"Is that why…" He dropped off and groaned as he closed his eyes. "It really was your wedding day, wasn't it?"

She nodded slightly, feeling as if finally one of her secrets was out.

"What did they want with you now?" His fingers dug into her arms, but she enjoyed the warmth of him holding her.

"With me? Nothing, but I was already eight months pregnant at the time." His fingers tightened a little more. "They wanted my… our child. He belonged to the sect. According to them, he was God's chosen child."

"Why in God's name didn't you come back to us?" She heard the rawness of his voice as his fingers tightened on her shoulders.

She closed her eyes and swayed. “There wasn’t time.”

The silence built between them. “And after you had our child?”

She shook her head as she closed her eyes to the pain. Her throat was raw, burning her. Opening her eyes, she looked up into his blue ones. “I need some water.”

He blinked and glanced around.

She almost smiled. “There’s a bottle in the cart.”

He nodded and then quickly walked back to the cart. She watched him closely. His kisses were the same, but different. He even moved differently than he had years ago.

By the time he made it back to her, her throat was dry for completely different reasons.

“I’d like to hear the rest,” he said, handing her the bottled water.

Taking a drink, she allowed the water to soothe the heat caused by watching him. Glancing down, she frowned at her watch.

“Maybe we can continue later. I have to pick up Reagan soon.”

She watched his eyebrows jump and saw a mixture of anger and excitement rush into his eyes.

“Would you like to…”

He took her shoulders. "Yes," he growled.

"Roman, I didn't mean to keep you away." She sighed, not really knowing what to say.

"Later." He took her hand and pulled her back to the cart. He drove with as much gusto as he had getting them there.

"I'm going to have to invest in one of these for dad," he said absentmindedly.

"How is he?" She peered at him from the corner of her eye. She tried to keep the guilty feeling from rushing in, but it always did when she thought about her adopted parents.

He glanced at her after slowing the cart down. "Mom died a short while after you left."

She nodded. "I know." She turned to him a little more. "I've followed all of you closely." Especially him, she thought, but she didn't say it out loud.

He pulled over and stopped the cart. "It was you." She watched his face closely.

"What? What was me?"

"At Mom's funeral. At the hospital when Cole was in his accident. Even at Cassey's wedding."

She shook her head slowly. "I…"

He looked like he was relieved. "What about opening day of Cassey's Boardwalk Bar and Grill?"

She blinked a few times and then swallowed the lump in her throat. He'd seen her. All the times she'd thought she'd gone unnoticed. He'd seen her. Nodding her head slightly, he chuckled.

"I told them I wasn't crazy." He smiled as he pulled back onto the road.

"How… You saw me all of those times?"

He glanced at her as they pulled back into the parking lot. "Sure." He shrugged. "I'd been looking out for you. Everyone had."

She didn't realize that tears had slipped down her face until he moved closer and used the back of his knuckles to gently wipe them away.

"You're family." His arms felt so good wrapped around her. She'd forgotten what it felt like. Being held. Letting go for a moment.

Chapter Six

Roman's hands were shaky and sweaty so he rubbed them on his shorts, trying to get his emotions under control. He sat outside the school with the woman of his dreams as he waited to see his son for the first time.

It was all like some dream. Any moment now, he expected someone to jump out of the bushes with cameras and tell him he was being punked.

"Why's the kid in summer school?" He felt a sickness in his stomach at the thought of the kid slipping in class.

She chuckled. "Because that's exactly where he wants to be." She turned to him. "It's not summer school, it's a summer reading program the school started a few years back to keep some of the advanced students from getting bored during the summer."

He blinked a few times. "So, he's pretty smart then?"

She smiled. "They want him to skip a grade."

He shook his head and frowned. "I tried that one year, remember."

She nodded and looked back to the school. "It's why I told them no."

He turned back to the school in time to watch a woman walk out the front doors and hold them open as a few kids came rushing out. Even if Missy hadn't told him, he would have known the second he saw the kid that he was the father.

He felt his eyes tear up again and had to blink several times so he could take in every detail about the kid walking towards him. His sandy hair was cut almost exactly like his had been at the same age. The kid's shoulders were slumped forward, mirroring the way that he walked all the time.

He was wearing khaki shorts and a blue button-up shirt with a worn pair of gray Chucks. When he saw Missy, he smiled quickly and then turned and waved to his teacher. It was like looking back into the past.

"When's his birthday?" he asked quietly before the kid got any closer.

She glanced at him and frowned. "July twentieth."

He sighed and nodded. "He'll be eight?"

She nodded, just as Reagan stopped in front of them.

"Hey." She leaned down and hugged him. "How was it today?"

Reagan shrugged his shoulders. Another move Roman knew too well. "It was okay. I finished *Holes*."

"Of course you did. What are you onto now?" She put her hand on his shoulder, pulling him a little closer.

He sighed, sounding a little bored. But Roman saw the sparkle in the kid's dark eyes and knew it too well. "Nothing good. Just…" His smile grew and he noticed he had his mischievous look down as well. "Percy Jackson!" He sounded excited.

"Which one?" Missy asked.

He rolled his eyes. "The best one of course." Then the kid's eyes moved over to him. He'd been standing so still, taking in everything, that he'd forgotten to breathe and actually felt light-headed.

"Who's that?" Reagan finally asked, leaning closer to his mom.

Missy's eyes met his, searching for answers.

"My name is Roman." He leaned down, not

looking up at Missy again. "I'm an old friend of your mother's." Making a quick decision, he smiled as he looked up at Missy. "I'll be staying with you and your mom for a while."

As she drove the short distance back to the shop, she kept sending glares his way.

The kid sat in the back of the car, enjoying the ride as much as Roman was. "When can I drive her?" he asked, reaching over to play with the tips of Missy's hair. She swiped his hand away quickly, and irritation crossed those eyes of hers, so he made sure to do it as often as he could.

"The way things are going? Never," she said between her teeth.

He chuckled. "Oh, come on. You probably wouldn't have ever purchased a car like this if it hadn't been for me."

He watched her eyebrows shoot up as she turned into the store's parking lot.

"Which is exactly why you won't get to drive it. I remember what you always said you'd do if you ever got your hands on one of these… beauties." She parked and turned off the engine. He already missed the hum and the vibration.

"We were kids." He smiled, remembering how he'd told her that he would win all the street races with it, and then he would take it out to Dolphin Bay to watch the submarine races with all the cheerleaders.

She turned to him and quickly glanced back at Reagan. "From the sounds of it… you still are." She turned as he laughed and got out of the car. "Now, if you don't mind, it looks like we're just in time for you to get back to work."

She nodded towards the ferry, which was pulling up to the dock again.

He got out and held in a groan since he'd wanted to spend as much time with Reagan as possible. Then he smiled. "Hey, kid, wanna come with me?"

Reagan glanced at his mom, then back at him. "Can I, Mom?"

She frowned and started to shake her head.

"Don't you trust me…?" The words "with our son" hung unsaid. His eyes bore into hers as she bit her bottom lip with worry. "Besides, Marv will be there," he added after a long pause.

She looked down at Reagan and smiled. "Would you like to go?"

The kid looked up at him with eyes just like his and nodded slowly. "Yeah, it beats sitting in the break room for a few hours."

Roman laughed and reached over and set his hand on the boy's shoulders. "We'll see you." He smiled as they started walking towards the docked ferry.

***

Missy looked out the window one more time as she chewed on her bottom lip.

"If you keep looking out the window, you'll never get that stuff unloaded," Jenny said from behind her.

She sighed and rolled her shoulders. "I know, but I can't help it."

"Listen." Jenny leaned closer so the few customers browsing the store didn't hear. "You have said that you know and trust the guy, right?"

She nodded slightly.

"Then what's the problem?"

"He's my son," she hissed. "You'll understand one day when you have your own. You never stop worrying about your kids. Even when they're with someone you trust."

Jenny laughed. "Stop worrying. Marv is looking out for them."

She nodded. "I know." She couldn't tell her friend that she wasn't worried that Roman would lose Reagan, or something bad would happen to her son. She was most worried about her son getting too attached to Roman.

He'd told her that he was going to stick around until she went back home with her, but that was something that could never happen.

Since she and Jenny had a ton of things to do before the end of the day, she was at least thankful that Reagan hadn't had to sit in the back room, bored. The kid needed to get out of the house more often. To say that he was a bookworm was an understatement.

He'd never climbed a tree or scraped his knee on a playground. Even during recess, his teachers told her that he spent his time sitting on a bench, reading or drawing.

Sure, there were activities they did together.

She would take him to the beach for nature hikes or picnics. Once, when he was six, they had gone to the state park and learned all about the flora from a guide. Reagan had been more interested in reading the guidebooks than actually seeing and touching the living plants.

Roman would have ended up just like that if it hadn't been for Marcus, who had dragged their butts all over Spring Haven. Marcus had talked the entire family into camping on the beach one summer night. Of course, he hadn't checked the weather and they'd been rained out, but still it went down as one of the best nights in her young mind.

Some of Marcus's adventurous nature had transferred to Roman over the years. The last night she'd had with him had been under the stars in the field behind their house.

Sighing, she remembered how he'd held her as they lay under the blankets he'd brought along.

"I can't believe you put all of this together," she said, looking over at Roman and the basket of food he'd brought along.

She'd worn one of her favorite jean skirts and white tops, along with an old pair of boots so she could rush through the fields and meet him at the spot he'd picked out. They sat near the edge of the lake behind their house, where no doubt the rest of their family was sitting around the television, arguing about what they were going to watch.

He smiled over at her as he opened the bottle of spring water and poured her some into the plastic glass. "I wanted tonight to be special."

She couldn't get over how handsome he looked in the moonlight. It was the end of the summer and his hair had turned a pale blond from its naturally darker tint. He'd let it grow out a little, which had caused the ends to have a slight curl. She loved running her fingers through it as they stole kisses.

She blushed remembering the first time his lips had brushed up against her own.

"Here," he said, handing her the glass. The water did little to quench the thirst she felt when she watched him. Her entire body felt like it was on fire and by looking at him, she knew he felt the same way.

"Roman." She glanced back towards the house.

"No," he broke into her thoughts. "Don't think about that." He frowned at her, setting her glass down and pulling her closer. "Not tonight. We're

just two people. Under the stars. Who want to be with one another." His eyes begged her to understand. So she nodded her head slightly.

When his lips covered hers, she instantly shut down the part of her mind that felt guilty. How could something so right not be right?

His fingers dug softly into her shoulders as he pulled her down onto the blanket. Her breath hitched when they moved slowly over her breasts, covering her until she felt her heart beat into his hands.

A moan escaped her lips when he trailed kisses down her neck, behind her ear, until she felt him unbuttoning her blouse. She arched for him, wanting to feel the warmth of his hand against her skin.

"Please," she begged, not understanding her own needs. "I need..."

"What?" His voice sounded low, a rumble next to her skin, causing goose bumps to rise over her exposed flesh. "Tell me what you need."

"You," she said, pulling him back up to her until his mouth covered her own. "Just you."

He shook his head as he looked down at her. "I don't want to stop this time." His eyes bore into hers.

"No." She smiled up at him, knowing that she'd been too afraid of being caught last time. This time, there was no one around. No reason to not

take what she wanted. What she needed. To show him how she felt. "Don't stop."

His eyes searched hers, and then he was kissing her again, his hands moving faster as she held onto him. She felt the need build in her when he hiked up her skirt and slid her panties down her legs. Reaching up, she helped him pull his shirt over his head and sighed as she traced her fingers over the lean, tan muscles. She'd always appreciated his body, had always desired it.

He scanned over her now. She was lying on the old blanket in only her white bra and jean skirt that was hiked up to just below her hips. His hands slowly traveled over her legs until they pushed the skirt up more. Her eyes closed on a moan when he covered her sex and started rubbing his thumb over her.

Her nails dug into the soft blanket when he pushed a finger gently into her as his other hand lay flat across her stomach. Her hips jumped as he dipped farther into her, circling, moving in a pattern that drove her slowly nuts.

"Roman," she cried out when she felt she could no longer hold out for him.

"Come," he said next to her ear. "Come for me."

She moaned and dug her nails into his bare shoulders as he covered her and slid slowly into her. She had never imagined anything being more perfect that that night under the stars on her seventeenth birthday.

Shaking her head clear of the memory, she finished unloading the last of the new stock and walked back over to the window to see the ferry returning on its last run for the night.

When she watched Roman and Reagan walk down the dock, laughing at something, her heart skipped a few beats.

She knew there was no way he wouldn't be part of their lives now. Even with the danger lurking, she knew she would do anything to keep the pair together. Especially when she watched Reagan's hand slip into Roman's as they walked. Her son had never trusted anyone else to get as close as she could tell the pair was even after only a few hours.

Rolling her shoulders, she tried to come up with the next steps, but nothing came to mind. She needed some more time to plan, to figure out a way out.

Instead, her mind kept replaying in slow motion that night so long ago under the stars.

Even her body betrayed her when the pair walked in the front door. Her heart skipped and she felt her face heat when his eyes settled on her.

"Well." She cleared her throat, which had gone dry. "How was it?"

"Mom!" Reagan rushed to her and hugged her around the waist. "Roman let me steer ol' Bertha."

"Ol'?" She chuckled as she looked over at Roman. "Of course you would name a ferry that."

He shrugged his shoulders and smiled over at her, causing her insides to quiver.

"Why don't you run back and get a juice and snack from the fridge." The kid was gone before she could finish her statement.

Roman laughed. "I guess we worked him a little too hard."

"No, he just likes eating." She turned back towards him. Her smile faltered when she noticed that he'd moved closer to her.

"Thank you," he said, taking another step closer.

"For?" She frowned a little.

"For letting him go along." He brushed a strand of her hair from her eyes. "He's perfect. So much like I was at that age."

She nodded, not sure what to say.

"We'll talk later, after the kid is asleep, about the rest." He nodded to the back room, where Reagan was. Roman's hand moved up and cupped her face, holding her still. "You owe me some more explanations."

She blinked a few times, trying to get her heart rate back in check. She'd missed how his dark eyes made her skin heat. How the feel of his hands on her made her moan. Memories of him sending her over the edge surfaced in her mind. Before she knew it, his hand was on her arm, holding her steady.

"Marissa?" His low voice broke into the memory.

"I…" She licked her lips, wanting. "I need to go close out." She turned and quickly walked behind the counter.

When she looked up again, he was walking past her to the back area. A few minutes later, she could hear Roman and Reagan laughing together.

How was she going to do this? Even their matching laughs did little to bring her spirits up. She knew they needed to be together, but something inside her told her it was impossible and fear surfaced each time she thought about a life with him.

She closed out more quickly than she ever had and didn't even bother making sure the drawer balanced with the computer. Shoving the bag of cash into the safe, she twisted the knob and walked to the back room, needing to get home quickly so she could regroup.

"Ready?" she asked Reagan.

"Mom, Roman says that he's going to cook us dinner," her son said, bouncing in the chair. "And that I can help him cook."

He'd maneuvered around her again.

Chapter Eight

He knew it was a dirty trick, but standing in Missy's kitchen with Reagan next to him as they waited for the water to boil together, he didn't care. Not when he was with his son. He would never feel guilty spending time with the boy. Especially after seven years had been taken from him.

He tried not to think about that when the kid was around since he knew he wasn't the best at hiding his emotions. At least not when it came to anger.

"So, next we'll need…" He glanced down at his little helper, who rushed over to the cookbook and frowned as he read the recipe.

"Garlic," he almost shouted. "Then cheese. We

melt the butter over a medium heat." Reagan looked up at him.

"Check." He stirred the melted butter.

"Then add milk and simmer for five minutes."

"Double check." He nodded his head, urging the kid to continue.

"Then add the garlic and cheese and whisk it quickly."

He rushed back over to the stove with the whisk in his hands.

"How about I add the cheese and you add the garlic?" He held up the two cups with the allotted amount of each in them.

"Okay, but I get to whisk. Right?"

Roman smiled. "If you think you can do it quick enough without spilling."

"Course I can." Reagan smiled up at him. "I'm a master chef."

Roman laughed and nodded. "Okay, how about we go on the count of three."

He enjoyed watching Reagan's dark head bent over the pot as he stirred as fast as his little arms could.

He'd spent most of his adult life helping boys Reagan's age come out of their shells. The only difference was, Reagan hadn't been abandoned and abused like he had as a child. Like so many of the kids that came to Spring Haven Home, a business he'd put all of his money and heart into growing.

How many nights had he lain awake as a boy, wishing that he had a place like that to run to? It wasn't until he'd almost died that he'd finally escaped the horrors and come to the Grayton's house. Then, everything had changed.

"Is it time to add the parsley and noodles?"

"Hmm," he said, looking down. "Maybe we should have a small taste test first?"

Reagan held up a spoon and smiled. When he did, Roman noticed for the first time that one of the kid's teeth was missing. Chuckling, he bent down. "I'm not sure. With that tooth missing, maybe I should have a taste too."

Reagan smiled. "I've got another one that's loose too." He put his finger into his mouth and wiggled the opposite tooth.

"Neat." Roman smiled. "Okay, taste testing in one, two—"

"Three!" Reagan shouted as he dipped his spoon into the creamy sauce.

They added the noodles to the sauce, though most of the noodles ended up on the countertop instead of the pan. As he helped Reagan serve the dinner, he thought he saw sadness cross Missy's eyes.

She had set the table with mismatched colored

plates and had poured herself a tall glass of red wine, which was almost gone by the time she started eating.

He'd been thankful that she'd had a case of beer in the garage. He had popped the top on one as he cooked and finished it up with the last bites of seconds.

"So, Reagan tells me that it was his idea to go to the summer reading class," Roman said, winking at the kid. "And that the class is planning a three-night trip to Disney in a week."

Missy's eyes narrowed as she looked at her son. "I've already told Reagan that we just don't have the money to send him this year."

Roman smiled. "Well, that's where Reagan and I worked out a schedule."

Her eyes turned to him and grew even narrower. "A schedule?"

He nodded, not meeting her eyes. "Sure. Reagan thinks that he's responsible enough to have a summer job. You know, instead of sitting in the back room of the store after school, he could help out around here. Maybe help stock the shelves, price items, clean up spills." He tilted his head and glanced at Reagan, who looked like he was holding his breath.

"Roman." Missy reached over and took Reagan's hand. "Reagan and I have already discussed—"

"Well, sure you have. But that was before I came around. You see, I'd be willing to pitch in some money. You know, maybe take some of it from my pay, since he'd be helping me out some."

"How would he be helping you out?" she asked, drinking the last of her wine.

"Well, for starters, he would be riding with me a couple times during the week on the ferry. You know, keeping me company. Running down and getting me a soda or helping me talk on the radio to the customers." He winked at the kid. Reagan was a natural when it came to talking about the area. He had even told a story about pirates that had sank their ship in the bay to avoid being captured. Everyone on the ferry had laughed and listened in.

"Why are you doing this?" Missy leaned a little closer and whispered.

"Because the kid deserves to go to Disney with his class." He shrugged.

"Please, Mom?" Reagan begged.

"Honey, why don't you run along and take your bath and get ready for bed while Roman and I have a chat?"

Reagan rolled his eyes, but before leaving the table, he picked up his dirty dishes and carried them slowly into the sink. "You won't leave until I come back out, will you?" Reagan asked.

"Nope. Can't get rid of me that easy, kiddo." He

messed up the kid's hair and smiled as Reagan skipped off down the hallway.

After taking their dishes to the sink, Roman rinsed them and placed them into the dishwasher. Then he turned around and noticed that Missy had leaned against the bar area, watching him.

"Why are you so set on him going on this trip?" she asked, taking another sip of a new glass of wine.

He shrugged again. "Maybe because it would give his mother and father a few days to discuss some things. Besides, the kid was super excited when he told me about it." He wiped his hands and walked over to her. "If it's a matter of money, don't worry, I'll cover the cost."

She shook her head. "No, it wasn't about the money."

"Then why didn't you want him to go?"

She blinked and looked away. "I have my reasons."

He sighed and put his hands on her shoulders lightly. When he felt her jump, he couldn't stop the smile. She'd always been a little off guard around him.

"Missy, let the kid go. He tells me four of his teachers are going, including his principal. He'll be in good hands."

She nodded. "Yes, I suppose. I'll think about it."

He chuckled. "Don't think too long. He says the forms are due tomorrow."

She closed her eyes and sighed. "Right."

"Besides, Orlando is only a few hours from here. If anything happened, we could be there in no time." He took a step closer, enjoying the feeling of her soft body pressed up against his.

She'd piled her blonde hair up in a clip at the top of her head. Several strands had fallen around her face, making him want to touch them and brush them away from her eyes. Her skin actually glowed in the soft light.

"Missy…"

"I'm done!" Reagan came running into the room, a large book in his hands. "Can Roman read me a book?"

He'd never moved so fast as he did jumping away from Missy. Instantly, he regretted it and tried to shelter the kid from seeing what her soft body had done to his.

Missy chuckled. "Sure, why don't you go settle in and I'm sure he'll be in in a few minutes." She moved in front of him.

***

Missy stood in the hallway and listened to Roman read to Reagan. She'd finished off her second glass of wine and felt her head circle a little. She normally didn't drink this much, but tonight, she doubted she could have handled being so close to Roman without it.

He'd stirred up a lot of emotions in her, as well as causing her body to react to his. Smiling, she leaned her head against the wall and remembered how his body had responded to her.

The smooth richness of his voice enticed her even further. She'd always loved the sound of it, the way it had caused her insides to vibrate.

When she heard his voice trail off, she opened her eyes and watched as he snuck out of their son's bedroom door. He noticed her and walked over and stopped right in front of her.

"Does he always drop off that quickly?" he asked softy.

She smiled and nodded. "He reminds me a lot of Cole in that area."

Roman chuckled. "You know, he still sleeps like that." He shook his head and took her hand and then tugged on her until she followed him back down the hallway into the living area. "Speaking of family…"

She sighed and felt the tension return to her shoulders. "Roman…" She sat down on the sofa and watched him follow her. "I can't return home."

"Well, at least you still think of it as home," he said dryly.

"I love our family." She turned, wishing she could explain everything.

"Then why are you here? Why not see them? Let them know you're alive." His dark eyes begged her so she avoided meeting them by looking down at her empty glass.

He reached for it and set it on the coffee table in front of them. "Missy." His hands took hers. "We miss you. Cassey spent the first two years after you left looking for you. She would drive around and look at open houses every weekend, hoping she'd find you in one of them."

She chuckled. "I'd forgotten."

"What? That you dreamed of buying an older home in Spring Haven, fixing it up and living happily ever after?"

She rolled her eyes. "It all sounds so childish now."

His fingers went under her chin, moving her until she looked deep into those chocolate eyes of his.

"We *were* children." It came out as a whisper. Somehow, he'd moved closer to her, so his breath mixed with hers. His musky scent was intoxicating. More so than the two glasses of wine she'd had already.

Something started building deep inside her chest, rolling downward until it rested in the soft spot between her thighs. She couldn't stop herself from wanting him. She'd never been able to.

His knee brushed up against hers, sending a

wave of desire slamming through her system. Why did her body always react to him like this?

"Yet, look at where you are. What you have. Isn't this what you'd dreamed of all those years ago?" he whispered.

Images flashed through her mind. Memories of her dreams. Almost every dream had included Roman. Right where he was now, leaning close to her, their bodies almost touching, his lips hovering over hers as his arms pulled her closer. Wasn't this part of that dream as well?

Her eyes were glued to his as she shook her head lightly. "I…" Before she could answer, his lips took hers in a kiss that was soft and yet so powerful that she felt as if her system had been jolted awake after years of hibernation.

He tugged on her shirt, pulling it up and over her head. Then his mouth moved lower, and she heard herself moan as his lips trailed over the peak of her breasts. Even with her thin bra on, she felt the moisture of his mouth, the heat from his tongue as it lapped at her skin, causing it to peak for him.

When her arms pulled him closer, she felt herself falling backwards onto the sofa. His body hovered over hers as he took the kiss deeper. Her shoulders pushed into the softness as the hardness of him moved against her chest.

She couldn't stop herself from running her nails up his arms to his shoulders. When he scraped his teeth against her jaw, she felt her entire body pulse.

She wanted him. Here. Now. Even after all of these years. She may have hidden herself from the truth, but there was no more denying it. She would always want him.

Chapter Nine

Roman couldn't stop his hands from shaking. Not when they were running over the most perfect skin he'd ever been given the pleasure of touching.

It was hard remembering that there was a kid in the next room. Their kid. Every time those words played over in his head, he felt anger start to boil. So, instead, he focused on Missy. He may not be able to completely let loose with the kid sleeping so close, but there were things he could do to pay her back for all those years she'd robbed him of.

Her shorts were loose, and when he tugged a little, he couldn't hide a smile when they slid down her legs easily. She looked up at him with big eyes as she bit her bottom lip.

"Roman…"

"Shhh." He covered her mouth with a finger. "It's okay, just let me enjoy." His eyes moved over her slowly, causing her to squirm under his intense stare. Her hands had dropped to her sides as he sat on his knees between her exposed legs. The tiny strip of yellow cotton covering her sex was no match when he used a finger to tear it aside.

He watched as her fingers dug into the sofa as her shoulders bounded off the cushion. He wanted to hear her scream his name but knew that was for next time, when they were alone.

His eyes burned her as he looked at her perfect body. Only her thin bra stood in the way of seeing all of her. In a few well-practiced moves, he had that barrier removed.

A goddess lay before him. Her shorter blonde hair pillowed around her face. Her lips were dark pink from his mouth as her eyes looked up at him with pure lust.

He wanted to take her. Hard. Fast. Forever. Instead, he ran a fingertip down her body slowly. Touching every part of her until her eyes closed as he slipped first one, then another finger into her heat. She was wet. Waiting for him. Welcoming him.

He felt his cock jump with want but held himself back. This wasn't about him tonight. This was about her. About showing her everything she'd missed. About showing her how long she'd kept everything from him. He was going to enjoy torturing her. Keeping her from her goal. Even now, her hips moved against his, wanting, begging.

He watched until her cheeks heated then pulled away. Then he ran his mouth from her chest bone to her pelvis, stopping at the dip between her thighs to lap and enjoy her taste. He skimmed his mouth over her soft skin as her fingers dug into his hair, pulling, holding him as she silently told him what she wanted.

Once again, he allowed her to build but not fall as he pulled away. Her eyes burned into his and a small crease formed between her eyebrows.

"Roman," she moaned, "I want…"

"I know what you want." His voice was low, almost like a growl. He shook his head, not trusting himself. The fact was, he wanted it too. He wanted to see her explode from his touch. Wanted to see her eyes go soft, her body tense as she came for him.

Spreading her legs wider, he ran a finger over her soft skin again and heard her sigh. Damn, she was making this almost impossible.

***

Each time Roman built her up, he moved away, causing her to become so sexually frustrated, she almost couldn't contain herself. If he didn't give her a release soon, she might just have to take what she needed herself.

Reaching up, she tugged on his shirt, until finally he leaned back and pulled it over his head, tossing it to the ground. When she sat up and ran her hands over his chest, his eyes closed with pleasure.

They had been children the last time they'd come together. So naive as they had created life. This time, she planned on taking her time exploring him, but he'd built her up too fast. All she could think about now was her own release.

When she moved to run her mouth over his chest, she heard his breath hitch and she smiled. She'd wondered if he was as moved as she was. Now she knew. As her mouth ran over his flat nipples, her fingers moved lower to the top of his shorts.

As she cupped him through his shorts and felt the hardness of him, she knew he was definitely as moved as she was. Maybe even more.

When she moved to slip her hand under his shorts, he pulled back and frowned down at her.

"Missy," he said, shaking his head. Then his eyes darted to the hallway and she knew instantly what he was afraid of.

"Roman, we can go to my room," she heard herself say boldly. She wanted too much to think through it at this point.

He closed his eyes and shook his head. "Not

unless you have protection." It was almost a growl.

She thought about it and frowned. She hadn't been with anyone since… "No," she whispered. "Fresh out," she said sarcastically.

He nodded. "Then, for tonight," he said, scooping her up quickly. "We'll just have to rein it in." He kissed her and started walking back towards her room. She buried her face into his shoulder when he walked quietly past Reagan's room.

Not until she heard her door shut and the lock being flipped did she open her eyes again. He was looking down at her, smiling as he laid her gently on her bed. "I like your space." He glanced around and then his eyes settled back on her.

He moved down to her, and she was grateful when his hands started moving over her again.

"You're so beautiful," he said next to her skin. His lips were quickly heating her back up. She'd changed so much since the last time they'd come together. Reagan hadn't been a small child by any means and her body had accommodated the almost nine-pound baby easily, but it had taken her a while to get her figure back. Even now, her hips had yet to go back down to their normal size.

He continued to talk to her softly, telling her how beautiful she was, how soft, the entire time he touched her, kissed her, causing small goose bumps to rise everywhere.

Her hands roamed him, feeling every muscle, enjoying feeling every beat of his pulse against her skin. When she felt herself building once more, she dug her heels into the mattress and held on but was once again disappointed when he pulled away.

"Roman," she begged, trying to keep him close to her by wrapping her legs around his hips and holding him to her.

He chuckled. "Easy." He kissed her neck, just below her chin. "I'm enjoying myself too much to rush."

"It's not rushing," she almost growled out. "It's torture."

He pulled back and smiled down at her. "Maybe you deserve a little torture. Especially after what you've put me through."

Looking deep into his eyes, she felt guilty all over again. An explanation was on her lips, but then he shook his head and frowned at her.

"No, not tonight." He reached up and cupped her face in his hands gently. His rough, calloused hands against her soft skin heated it even further. "That's for later."

"Then… why are you torturing me?"

His smile was fast. "Maybe I enjoy watching you squirm."

She looked into his eyes and could see sadness there, but she could also see desire. Deciding two could play this game, she quickly rolled and didn't stop until he was beneath her. Pinning his arms down to his sides, she straddled him. The fact that she was completely naked now, while he still had his shorts on, caused her some distress. So, bending down, she tugged until finally he was as naked as she was.

Her eyes slowly moved over his entire body. He'd been a boy the last time, and she'd been so shy that she hadn't enjoyed looking. Now, however, she let her eyes take him all in. Every glorious inch of him told her that he was a man instead of the boy she'd fallen in love with so many years ago.

She felt doubt creeping in, so before she could back out, she leaned down and ran her fingers and mouth over him.

His fingers dug into her cotton comforter as his hips jerked when she took him fully into her mouth.

"Missy, my god," he groaned, his hands going into her hair. She loved the taste of him, the soft skin over steel. She took her time, pleasing him as she learned every inch of him.

When his hips started moving, she leaned back and looked down at him with a smile.

"It doesn't feel good, does it?" she asked, running her hands over his thighs.

For an answer, he flipped her over until she lay underneath him again. This time, his fingers dove into her, and she knew he wouldn't stop.

***

He couldn't stop if he wanted to. Not after she'd tortured him to the brink, till he knew what it was like, needing so very much. His fingers took what he wanted, gave her what she needed until she lay below him, lax and sated.

Then he lay down next to her and tried to control his own breathing as his mind rushed over the events of the last forty-eight hours. Her fingers kept circling his chest until finally, she moved over him.

She smiled down at him and he tensed for just a moment before her lips covered his. He had forgotten how soft she felt over the years. How beautiful she'd been. Even now, looking up at her, he didn't want to close his eyes in case he missed any little detail about her. The way her hair fell around her face or how her eyes heated when she ran her hands over his chest.

When she dipped her head lower, he watched as she gripped his length and started a slow movement around him, causing a groan to escape.

"I had my turn," she almost purred. "Now, it's yours." Then she was taking him to places he'd only dreamed about since the first time he'd touched her so many years ago.

He hadn't even known he'd been missing anything with other women he'd seen during her absence. They all paled in comparison to the way he felt when he was around her. The way she'd always made him feel. Safe. Like he was home.

He must have dozed off for a while after she'd snuggled next to him. When he cracked his eyes open, he could see the top of her head resting on his chest. Reaching down, he covered them with a blanket and smiled when she buried herself closer to him.

He could just make out the light coming through her blinds and knew that his time holding her would be limited. He had plans to make sure that he stayed right where he was for the rest of his time there, or at least until he convinced her to return home for a visit. After that, he didn't know what the future held, only that now that he had found his family, there was no way he was letting them go again.

The morning was something dreams were made of. Well, his dreams anyway. He helped Missy with the mundane chores of getting an almost eight-year-old ready for a day at school.

He even cooked eggs and toast while she was in the bathroom, getting dressed. He found it incredibly sexy that even after last night, she still blushed around him when he watched her walk into the bathroom naked. Of course, he had had to spend a few minutes thinking about something else before he'd finally emerged from the bedroom.

With the help of Reagan, he talked Missy into filling out the forms and writing a check for

Reagan's trip to Orlando. He had to admit, he and the kid had made a great team when convincing her.

He knew he needed to tread lightly about telling the kid he was his father. How did one go about bringing up the topic?

By the time they drove her car to the school, he'd made the decision to tell the kid later that night over ice cream. But after watching Missy kiss the boy goodbye, he started having his doubts.

"Don't," she said without looking over at him as she waved to Reagan. The kid turned at the door and looked back, a slight frown on his lips, until he finally smiled and waved back.

"What?" Roman asked, turning to her. "Ask to drive the car?"

She chuckled, but shook her head from side to side.

"Roman, even after all these years, I can tell you have been deep in thought."

He shrugged his shoulders. "Just what do you think I'm deep in thought about?"

"Reagan." She crossed her arms over her chest and scowled at him. "Telling him about you."

He frowned. "He has a right to know."

"I'm not questioning that." She walked around and got behind the wheel. "I just think we should take it slow."

"Slow?" He almost growled the word. "Eight years isn't slow enough?" he asked, stopping himself from slamming the car door.

She turned and glared at him as he pulled out of the parking lot.

"I had my reasons," she said, not looking in his direction.

"And? When will I be invited to hear your explanations?"

She sighed and rolled her shoulders. "When I'm ready." She glanced at him after saying this.

"What about me? Don't I get a say in this? After all, you're the one who took my voice away for eight years."

"Roman." She pulled to a stop in the parking lot of the store. "Just give me a little more time."

He was boiling inside, but the look in her eyes convinced him to give her the time she needed. Releasing the breath he'd been holding, he nodded slightly.

"Marv wanted to watch you for a day before handing over the ferry to you." She nodded to where Marv stood on the doc, waiting for him.

"Will I see you later?" he asked.

She nodded. "I was planning on going to the island for lunch, if you'll join me?"

He smiled and then quickly pulled her across the seat and covered her mouth with hers.

"I plan on staying at your place, you know. And tonight, we won't have to hold back," he whispered next to her ear. He thought he felt her shiver and hoped it was with anticipation.

Chapter Ten

Roman's words played over in her head the rest of the morning. *"Tonight, we won't have to hold back."*

Just the thought that he'd held back any last night sent heat spreading throughout her entire body. She had been so absentminded while daydreaming about last night that she'd started stocking the orange juice on the center aisle instead of in the refrigerators. She'd caught herself before anyone had noticed and had quickly restocked the fridge while blushing.

But the more she thought about it, the more his words took on a different meaning to her. She was the one still holding back from him. He'd walked into a sticky situation and had blindly believed everything without getting any answers. Before she did anything else, she realized she had to tell him everything.

She pulled out a grilled half chicken from the rotisserie oven and packed up her small cooler with cheese, crackers, and sodas. Then she went to wait at the end of the dock for the ferry to return.

Marv had assured her that he'd take most of the days for the rest of the month, but there were at least a handful that Roman would have to fill in. John and Bob had been excited to fill in full time until Jenny could hire two more replacements.

She knew the time had come to finish telling Roman her story. Actually, that's why she'd set the lunch date. She kept telling herself not to back down, but part of her still wanted to run and hide. Nothing was more important to her than her son's safety and Roman finding her had been the biggest breach possible.

When the ferry pulled up, she found it hard to smile and wave at Roman as he stood in the bridge after docking. She waited until everyone else had left before climbing on board. There were only two cars heading back to the island during the lunch trip, which at this time of year was slow. But she knew that things would be speeding up during the weekend with the holiday coming.

"Hey." Roman smiled at her and pulled her closer in for a light kiss. Missy watched Marv's bushy eyebrows jump upward.

"I have our lunch." She nodded to the cooler. "I packed a slice of Jenny's cheesecake for you, Marv," she said in hopes of discouraging her employee from telling everyone about the kiss.

She smiled when his eyebrows lowered.

"Looks like we might get some rain later tonight," Marv said, taking the container of the large slice of cake from her.

She nodded and turned back to Roman. "Care to go out on deck and get some fresh air with me?"

He smiled. "As long as you promise me you brought some of that cheesecake for us."

She chuckled and nodded.

"Then lead the way." He waved his hand after opening and holding the door for her.

When she walked out on the deck, the warm breeze hit her. Marv was right; she could almost smell the rain in the air. By nightfall, everything would be wet.

When Roman stopped beside her, he took her shoulders into his hands and turned her until she looked at him. "Looks like you have something pretty heavy on your mind." His fingers played with the ends of her hair. She wanted nothing more than to just be held by him for the rest of the day. Instead, she nodded slightly.

"I think it's time I told you everything." Her

eyes met his and she could see some relief in them.

"Here?" He waited.

She shook her head from side to side, sending her hair into her eyes until she looked down at his chest. "During lunch," she whispered.

He pulled her closer and she easily rested her head on his chest. "Thank you." His voice rumbled in her ear.

She pulled back slightly. "Don't thank me." She felt her stomach almost roll. "I don't deserve your thanks." Her head was spinning just at the thought of what he was getting himself into by being with her.

He nodded slowly. "Okay." He drew the word out and she sighed deeply.

"I'm sorry." She closed her eyes and felt her head pounding. "Let's just save the talking for after we eat."

He nodded again then pulled her back into his arms and kissed her forehead. "Whatever it is, we can work through this together."

She closed her eyes on the hurt, knowing that that would never be possible.

***

Roman liked to think he was a patient man. After all, it had taken him over eight years to track Missy down. But as he sat on the picnic table overlooking the sugar sand beach, he felt his patience finally wearing down.

Missy nibbled on her chicken and picked at it with a plastic fork instead of picking it up and digging into it like he had. It looked to him as if she was postponing the conversation as long as she could.

He finished his plate quickly and watched her pull out a pan with the cheesecake wrapped inside. After cutting him a large piece, she set her fork down and pushed her almost full plate aside. He'd only taken a few bites of his cake, when her eyes moved up to his. Setting his fork down, he waited.

"I found my… well, technically, he's my grandfather on my mother's side."

"What?" he asked.

She repeated her statement so he shook his head. "I don't understand."

She stood up and walked towards the surf, holding herself tightly. He followed close behind her, wanting to touch her but deciding against it. When she sat down in the sand, he moved beside her, their knees brushing slightly.

"Just before Reagan was born, I was scared and running. I'd just escaped the cult…"

"You had to escape the cult?" He frowned, turning towards her.

"They kidnapped me." Her voice was low, causing him to lean a closer. "After my mother visited me." She glanced over at him.

"I remember, she came up to the house and asked to speak to you."

She nodded.

"We turned her away." He frowned, remembering the junkie woman who had shown up. She'd had needle marks in her arms and a scared look in her eyes.

She sighed and rested her elbows on her knees. "She found me the next day, when I was leaving school." He felt anger boiling deep inside. "She'd left the CoF—the Council of Friends—a few years back and had gotten back involved in drugs." She shivered. "Anyway, someone from the family had tracked her down and told her to visit me. She told me that they claimed it was time I came back and fulfilled my obligations to the family. So, that night, after catching what I thought was you and Susan Shaffer, I left Spring Haven. I was so young and stupid that I rented an apartment in Tallahassee under my birth name."

"Marissa Collins?" he questioned.

She shook her head no. "That's what Lilly told the Grayton's my name was. To protect me." She rested her chin on her arms. "I've used a few names until I came here. Wright, Collins, but my birth name was Marissa Smith. I'm one of sixteen Smith's born into the Kevin Smith cult."

"Kevin Smith is your father?"

She shrugged her shoulders. "At least he seems to think so. It's hard to know who belongs to whom in a polygamous cult. In the Council of Friends, every child takes the leader's name." She glanced down at her hands. "And every leader takes the last name of Smith. The compound is just outside of Tallahassee."

"I thought those cults were only in Utah?" He frowned.

She shrugged her shoulders and looked back up at him. "Several larger groups broke off a few decades ago. Some settled in Colorado and others even farther away. The CoF moved near the Florida border. That's where I was born and raised until Lilly helped me escape on my wedding day and brought me to the Grayton's."

"Why would they kidnap you?" He reached out and took her hand in his.

She looked down at the joined hands and shrugged her shoulder. "They didn't want me. My father"—by the tone of her voice, he could tell that she hated using that term—"claimed that he'd received a message from God that I was pregnant. I had just found out myself less than a week earlier. He claimed that his first grandchild was to become their next prophet." Roman growled and she turned towards him. "After I escaped, I was pretty much living on the street. I had some money…" She shook her head. "I'd stolen it from the CoF as I escaped. But it wasn't enough. Just before Reagan was born, an older man came to the clinic I'd visited and found me. He claimed to be my mother's father. He'd been watching the compound for years, hoping his daughter would change her mind. She'd foolishly joined the cult to try and clean her life up. She was heavily into drugs in her youth." She sighed and hugged herself. "He brought me to Carrabelle, where he'd been living for a few years. He'd purchased Dog's Landing. He told everyone he'd hired me on and we changed my name once more."

"How do you know you're safe here?" He looked off towards the mainland. Thoughts of rushing to gather Reagan flooded his mind.

A chuckle escaped her. "I don't. But Doug, my grandfather, did everything in his power before he died a few years back to make sure they wouldn't find us again."

He shook his head, wanting to know more, but he had too many other questions that needed to be answered first. "Why didn't you contact me? We would have…"

She stopped him by putting a hand on his arm. "Because they knew about you. About the Graytons. Remember? When they kidnapped me, they claimed that if I ran…" She released a slow breath as she shook her head. "They wouldn't stop until they had Reagan." She leaned closer. "Roman, these are some scary people. They have money. Lots of money, weapons, and power. More than most drug lords in Mexico."

"If they knew about us, why didn't they come after you all those years ago?"

"They don't want me. I'm an apostate. I abandoned my church, my leaders. No matter how young I was when I left, I belonged to Satan the moment I stepped foot outside the compound."

"Then why our son?" he asked, shaking his head.

"It was determined on my second birthday that my first born would be a son and would one day rise to become their leader and guide CoF into the promised land. Everything they are, everything they've worked for over the last few decades rests on our son's shoulders. Or so they believe."

"I…" He shook his head, unsure of what to say. The only thing he knew for certain was that there was no way in hell the CoF was getting their hands on Reagan.

Standing up, he dusted the sand from his hands, then reached down and helped her up.

"I promise you, they will never get a chance to lay a finger on our son." His eyes burned into hers until she nodded slightly.

She believed him with every ounce of her being. She just hoped he'd never have to prove it.

***

As she watched the land disappear as they rode back to the mainland on the ferry, Missy shivered remembering her time in the compound when she'd been pregnant with Reagan. She couldn't imagine their son enduring something like that. Being locked up, watched, beaten.

She'd been born on the compound and had escaped it along with Lilly's help so many years ago. She knew of its weaknesses and its strongholds. But over the years, things had changed. Even during the time between when she'd escaped as a child and escaped eight years ago, so much had changed.

They had added electricity to their security walls so that anyone trying to climb under or over the high fences would be shocked. She shivered at the thought of what they had added in the time she'd been there last.

She was sure that escaping them twice had been a fluke. If they ever found Reagan, she feared there would be no escape.

"Roman, I know you want to tell Reagan about us," she said, turning towards him. "But, I don't think he's ready."

Roman tilted his head and looked at her. "Are you having a problem with him being ready or you being ready?"

She sighed and leaned a little more on the railing as she watched the water below. "I suppose it's me that isn't ready." She turned away from the view and leaned backwards against the railing. "I've been a single parent his entire life. It's going to be a shock hearing about you. Hearing my past." She closed her eyes against the fear.

"He seems like a pretty smart kid," Roman said, running his hand over her shoulders. "Something tells me he's going to have a lot easier time with it than you think."

She thought about it and nodded, trying to rein in her fears. "Do you want me…"

He stopped her by shaking his head. "No, we need to do this together." She nodded and moved easily into his arms. When he leaned down and kissed her, she realized she no longer cared who saw them together.

Chapter Eleven

By the time they picked up Reagan, he'd talked Missy into taking the rest of the evening off from work. Marv had even agreed to finish up the rest of the runs for the night.

After picking up Reagan from school, Missy had shocked Roman by tossing him the keys to the car.

"Really?" His eyebrows shot up. She'd smiled and nodded. After helping Reagan into the back seat, making sure the kid snapped on his seat belt, he climbed behind the wheel of his dream car with his dream family.

Checking the rear mirror, he asked, "What do you say to some pizza tonight?"

"Yeah!" Reagan jumped up and down, pumping his arms in the air like he was on a roller coaster. He stopped when his mother turned around and looked at him. "Can we, Mom?" His bottom lip pulled out in a pout.

She sighed, looking over at Roman, then smiled and nodded. "Why not."

He felt like peeling out of the parking lot, but with Reagan in the back and Missy sitting beside him, he pulled out at a normal speed.

Instead of heading into town and the local pizza place along the water, he took a left and headed down to Cape San Blas and Port St. Joe.

Joe Mama's Wood Fired Pizza, a ma and pa run joint, sat less than a block from the water's edge and had some of the best pizza along the coast. The typically hour-long drive took even longer since he ended up cruising and enjoying the coastal drive.

It was funny—most of his teen years had been spent dreaming about racing the very car he was driving. But now that he finally has gotten behind the wheel of one, he had too much respect for the machine to go fast.

"We've never eaten here," Reagan said as Roman opened the back door to help him out.

"Well, kiddo, sometimes you just have to try new things." His eyes burned into Missy's a little and he was pleased when he saw her cheeks flush.

When he opened her door, she looked around the small town. "We've been here before." It was more of a statement than a question.

"My eleventh birthday." He smiled and nodded. "Had ice cream over there." He frowned when he realized it was now a frozen yogurt place.

She chuckled, causing him to glance down at her. "Maybe they'll have mint chocolate chip for you." She patted his arm and then walked over to where Reagan stood waiting for them.

He was very pleased that she'd remembered his favorite flavor. Walking over, he took her hand in his and walked into the pizza place. The smells hit them full force and they all sighed and smiled as they were seated.

"Wow, look at how they flip that," Reagan said, pointing to the man behind the counter who was tossing and twirling the pizza dough around.

He chuckled. "Haven't you ever seen a pizza dough twirler before?" he asked.

Reagan shook his head. "I've read about them." The kid's eyes were glued to the motion. "What happens if he drops it?"

Roman laughed. "I suppose he'd have to throw that dough away."

Reagan shook his head. "Seems like a waste."

"Oh? What would you do?"

The kid shrugged his shoulders. "Bake it and

feed it to some hungry dogs."

Roman's eyebrows shot up. "Good idea."

Throughout their dinner, the kid continued to amaze Roman with his unique way of looking at the ordinary. By the time their pizza was gone, he was seriously questioning if he had any room for dessert, but since he'd promised himself that he'd tell Reagan over ice cream, he walked across the block with Missy and Reagan close to him.

He could tell as they picked their flavors that Missy was getting nervous. Her eyes kept darting towards the door like she was hoping to escape somehow.

When they walked back out to the front and sat under the patio, he decided he would wait until Reagan was done with his yogurt. But, realistically, he needed to settle his nerves a little before blurting it out.

For some reason, the scene from Star Wars kept playing over and over in his head. *Reagan, I am your father.* Just didn't seem fitting.

Finally, when they were all done, he took a deep breath and grabbed Missy's hand in his.

***

Missy sat silently, waiting for the bomb to drop. She could feel Roman's hand shake in hers and when he glanced at her, she saw fear in his eyes. She watched him swallow slowly.

"Reagan." His voice sounded grim. He cleared

his throat and tried again. “Your mother and I have something we need to discuss with you.”

“I already know,” her son said, looking down at his hands on the table.

“You…?” Roman blinked a few times and then looked at her for help.

“What do you know, honey?” She leaned forward and took his smaller hand in hers.

Reagan’s brown eyes moved up to Roman’s. “I know that you’re my father,” he blurted out. “I know that Mom took me away from you and hid me.” He blinked and she was horrified to see a tear escape his eyes.

“Oh, honey!” She rushed closer to him and picked him up. “I didn’t mean to take you away from him. Roman never knew about you until yesterday.” She pulled his chin up with her finger until he looked at her. “I swear.”

He nodded and swallowed. “Why?”

Now it was her turn to cry. She looked over to Roman for help. His eyes were glued to his son’s. “Your mother did what she thought was best at the time. She didn’t want to keep us apart.” He walked over and picked Reagan off of her lap like he weighed nothing and held onto him while tears slipped down his face.

“You’re okay with this?” Roman asked after a while.

Reagan nodded his head and wiped the tears with his shirt. “I always wanted a dad.”

“How did you know?” Roman asked after a moment.

“Duh!” Reagan rolled his eyes and chuckled. “We look so much alike. Even Mrs. Miller knows.”

Roman smiled and hugged him again. “Then, you didn’t really need the ice cream?” he teased, wiping the kid’s tears then his own.

Reagan’s face turned a little red. “Course I did. I’m a growing boy.”

Missy laughed and rushed over to hug the pair of them.

Her mind whirled through the day’s events as Roman drove slowly back to Carrabelle. The rain had started just after they’d gotten back into the car. Roman had pulled over on the side of the road and put up the top.

“I can look into getting a new back window.” He nodded towards the sheet of plastic she’d had taped up ever since she’d purchased the car.

She shrugged her shoulders. “I hardly have the top up anyway.”

He chuckled and glanced at her. “It’s a shame too.” Then he looked back to the backseat of the car where Reagan was fast asleep, his head resting on his book bag. “He’s pretty amazing.”

She glanced over her shoulder and nodded. "He always has been."

"I know it doesn't matter much, but I don't really want people in town thinking I was a deadbeat dad."

She frowned, looking down at her hands as she nodded. "I understand." She did understand. After all, Carrabelle was important to her. Almost as important as Spring Haven.

He reached over and took her hand. "Thanks."

She felt her heart flutter when he looked at her. For the rest of the drive home, he kept hold of her hand, rubbing his thumb over her skin in slow circles. Which only reminded her of how he'd touched her the night before.

By the time they pulled into her garage, the light rain had turned into a small monsoon. He was thankful that she had a cover from her garage to her back door as he carried the sleeping Reagan inside. The boy slept all through Missy pulling off his shoes and jeans.

When she tucked the blanket over him, he snuggled in and rolled over.

"He's a good sleeper," she whispered as she shut his door. When she turned around, he took her hand and walked with her until they stood out on the front porch. When he dropped her hand, he walked over and stood against the railing, watching the rain pour down.

"Your gutters need cleaning," he said absentmindedly.

She glanced up and noticed that the rain was pouring out of several spots. "I have a guy that does that once a year. I'll call…"

"I can do it." He turned to her, a slight frown on his lips.

She nodded and wrapped her arms around herself.

"Before…" He shook his head and took a deep breath. "Before we go any farther, I need you to know that I'm not going anywhere. I plan on being in Reagan's life from here on out."

She nodded again and walked over to the railing to stand next to him. "I wouldn't want it any other way."

He turned to her and ran his hand up her arm, pulling her a little closer.

"That means that he's part of our family, as well."

Her heart skipped a beat. "I won't do anything to jeopardize his safety."

He nodded. "Neither would the family."

She shook her head. "No, you don't understand. We can never go back to Spring Haven."

He frowned and pulled her closer. "We'll find a way."

She felt tears rolling down her face. For too long, she'd wished to return home, but Reagan was too important and she had never wanted to chance being discovered. She didn't know if her family… if the CoF was still looking for Reagan. She'd prayed for years that they would just give up, but something told her they hadn't.

Roman's visit had only heightened her fear. She'd stopped looking over her shoulder years ago, believing that Doug had done everything to protect them here.

But fear kept surfacing now. If Roman had found her, how easy would it be for the CoF to?

"Roman?" She pulled back and looked up at him. "How did you find me?"

He chuckled and shook his head. "It wasn't easy." She waited. Finally, he walked over and sat down on the porch swing and patted the spot next to him. She walked over and sat next to him. He kicked off, sending the swing swaying. She enjoyed his warmth when his arm went over her shoulders and pulled her closer.

"Do you remember Liam?"

She blinked a few times, and then a memory of a tall, skinny, red-haired boy who had always been a big joker popped into her mind. "Freckle face?"

Roman chuckled and nodded. "He's stationed at Port St. Joe air base. One weekend, Liam and his new wife, Barb—you went to school with her—"

"Barb Kensington?"

He nodded and smiled.

"Anyway, they wanted to get away for the weekend and decided a short trip to Dog Island would be just the thing."

She closed her eyes and sighed, knowing the rest.

"He called me immediately, since he knew I'd had a PI looking for you for years."

She gasped and looked at him. "You have not."

He nodded, his eyes turning even darker. "Did you think we—that I—wouldn't look for you?"

She felt his warmth pulling her closer. "I…" She shook her head.

His hand came up to brush a strand of her hair away from her face. "I'll always look for you," he said softly. "I'll always find you," he whispered just before his lips rested over hers.

Chapter Twelve

Roman wanted to go slow. After last night, he'd made sure to come prepared and planned on spending time enjoying himself while he made sure she enjoyed herself just as much.

Even as his lips traveled over hers, he could feel himself wanting to take what he wanted. He'd come onto the porch instead of going back to her bedroom to try to slow himself down.

The sound of the rain grew softer as his hands roamed over her body. He'd noticed slight changes in her since they'd been kids but had marveled at every curve, every dip she now carried as a woman.

"Missy," he spoke against her lips. "You're

making it very hard for me to go slow.

She giggled against his neck. "Then don't." Her hands gripped his shoulders, pulling him closer. Her breath was hot on his skin, turning him on even more. Finally, after she started tugging on his shirt, he stood up, lifting her easily into his arms, and marched them through the house quietly.

When he kicked her door shut behind them, he felt a wave of desire hit him full force. She was looking up at him with her caramel eyes full of lust. Several steps later, he was following her down to the bed where their mouths slanted over one another's again. This time, when clothing hit the floor, he made sure to pull out the packages of condoms he'd stored in his back pocket.

Missy smiled when she saw that he'd brought more than one. "You came prepared." He nodded, since his throat had gone dry just looking at her.

"I did, too." She reached over and opened her top drawer to her nightstand. "We sell them at the store." She nodded to the box of condoms sitting inside.

He smiled. "I know, where do you think I got these. You'll have some explaining to do to Jenny tomorrow."

She giggled. "Explaining?" She smiled. "More like bragging."

He laughed as he pulled her back underneath him. "Then I suppose I'd better make this good."

She moaned when his lips covered hers. Her fingers dug into his skin as he trailed his mouth lower to cover her breasts one at a time.

"Roman, I need…" She pulled his hair until he was back at her lips. "Now." He watched her bite her bottom lip.

"You have me so hot." He almost growled it. "I can't decide what's what." He slipped on a condom and settled in between her thighs. "Look at me." He waited until her eyes locked with his before plunging into her.

When she threw her head back and moaned, he almost lost control. She was tight and wet and he realized he should have taken it slower. But as her legs wrapped around his hips, he was powerless to her silent demands.

Their lips locked and their tongues dueled as his hips pumped quickly. His fists dug into the sheets as he tried to maintain some hold on his control. Then she ran her tongue over his neck and nipped at the spot just below his ear and he went blind with lust.

***

Missy held on and enjoyed the ride until she felt his control slip, then she couldn't maintain a hold on her own control. Her thighs tightened around him as he continued to slide in and out of her quickly. Her inner muscles stretched to welcome him, even thought it had been years.

When he rained hot kisses down on her face, she gripped his hips and threw her head back in pure ecstasy.

Her heart felt like it was trying to jump out of her chest. He'd fallen down on her and covered her body with his warm one. They were slick with sweat and as the evening air cooled around them, she shivered.

He rolled and pulled the comforter over them as she snuggled closer to him.

"Why didn't you tell me it had been a while?" he asked, slowly running his hands over her.

"How do you know?" She frowned into the darkness of the room and heard him chuckle. "Well?" she said after a while. She propped her head on her elbow and looked in his direction, but it was a little too dark to see him.

"Are you telling me that it hasn't been?" he asked.

She heard him moving and almost screamed when the light on her nightstand flipped on. Its brightness was blinding. She reached for the sheets and covered herself while he chuckled.

"One of the other hints that it's been a while." He smiled and played with the sheet near her chest.

Instead of answering, she shrugged her shoulders.

"How long?" It was almost a whisper.

For some reason, she couldn't meet his eyes.

"Missy?" His finger stopped playing with the sheet and moved up to under her chin, then nudged it until she met his eyes.

"I've only slept with one man in my life." She raised her chin more.

He couldn't stop the smile as he pulled her closer. This time the kiss was soft, and he poured every emotion into it, hoping she could pick up on them.

When her hands moved to his shoulders and pushed him back onto the bed, he let her hover over him, her thighs trapping his hips to the mattress as she ran her hands and mouth over his chest and arms. Then she moved lower and he wondered just how long he could tolerate her soft touches until he rolled her over and took her hard and fast again.

"You're so soft, yet hard." She smiled up at him, making him want to laugh out loud from the glory of the feeling of her touching him. "Does this feel good?" she asked, running her fingers over his length.

His eyes slid closed and he nodded, swallowing the lust she was causing.

"And this?" Her fingers circled the head of his cock.

His eyes opened and locked with hers. "You're playing with fire," he said in a low voice.

"I'm just getting familiar." She smiled down at him as she ran her fingers over him some more. "I've never had the chance to explore a man before."

He took a couple deep breaths and nodded. "Do your worse."

She chuckled and dipped her head. "Did you like it when I…" Her lips brushed against his cock, causing it to jump in her hand.

"More than you know." His eyes closed as he concentrated on anything other than the way she was making him feel.

When she took him fully into her mouth, he fisted his hands on the sheets again and tried to convince himself that he could hold out just a little longer.

When she reached over and took another condom from her nightstand, he relaxed back and watched her take her time slipping the protection on him.

Then she hoisted herself up on her knees and reached between them. Her fingers brushed up against him as she positioned him and slid slowly down until she was fully impaled once more. He moaned at the feeling of her tightness wrapped around him.

His hands moved to her hips, begging her to move slowly this time. She was leaning over him, her hair falling around her face as she watched him.

"Tell me what you like," she whispered.

His eyes met hers. "You," he said, his voice raw with emotion. He watched her eyes darken, and then she was moving over him, her hips rotating in small circles.

His eyes closed slowly as he threw his head back, his jaw going taut as he concentrated on her every movement. This time it was his turn to beg.

His fingers dug into her soft hips until he finally forced her to slide up and down on him. Her hands braced on his chest as she moved up and down over him more quickly.

His hips continued to pump as she knelt over him, until she threw her head back and cried his name. He rolled them until she was beneath him and continued to move inside her until he felt her tighten once more around him, then he joined her and let himself go.

***

When he woke again, the bed next to him was empty. After looking at the clock, he groaned at the early hour. Even working for his brother Marcus at his construction company, he'd never woken up this early.

When he heard the shower running in her bathroom, he smiled and crawled out of the bed.

She had one of those large showers that was all tile and glass, so when he opened the bathroom door, she glanced over at him and smiled. When she noticed that he was naked and very hard, her smile slipped a little.

Without saying anything, he moved across the room and stepped into the shower with her. When their lips met, her fingers dove into his hair and held him close.

He ran his hand over her soapy body as he walked her back until her shoulders were against the tile. He pulled her leg up until she was fully exposed for him. Propping her leg on the tile seat, he slid quickly into her, causing her to gasp into his mouth.

"I can't seem to get enough," he said against her neck. "I don't think I ever will." He kissed her again.

When her leg started to slip, he turned her until she was leaning on the seat, her tight little rear facing him. He took hold of her hips and pumped into her until he felt her break, then continued until his own release took him quickly.

***

"I've never done that before," she said, glancing over at him as she dried off from their shower.

He chuckled and looked at her. "Honey, from the sounds of it, you haven't done a lot."

She blushed, wishing she could take her words back. He walked over and wrapped his arms around her, smiling down at her.

"Don't be embarrassed. I'll just have to take my

time showing you everything." He drew out the last word as he kissed her. "Trust me, I'm a very good teacher." He kissed her one last time.

"We'll have to have a talk about how you became so… educated." She watched his eyes and saw the moment he understood her meaning. But before he could answer, Reagan knocked on her bedroom door.

"Mom! I'm hungry." She chuckled and nodded.

"Saved for now."

She narrowed her eyes at him as she walked out to get dressed.

Over the next few days, they fell into a pattern. Roman moved his bag of clothes from the hotel and settled into the two drawers she'd cleaned out for him in her dresser. On Marv's days off, he worked on the ferry. The other days he helped out with deliveries, stocking, or with Bob and John on the other boat. Once, he'd even gone with the guys on the fishing boat.

He'd filled her freezer with red snapper and grouper, enough that she'd have fish for the rest of the year. He'd even taken the time to fix a few things around the house.

He'd cleaned the gutters the next sunny day and had shocked her by spending a whole day working on her car. He'd replaced the duct-taped window with a glass one and had changed the oil and rotated the tires.

She could tell he'd enjoyed every minute of it. Reagan had been by his side the entire time, handing him tools and learning all about cars from his father.

It had been such a great moment that she'd snapped a few pictures on her phone of the greasy pair.

By the time Fourth of July rolled around, everyone in town knew that he was living with her and Reagan. She'd had a few questions to answer from Jenny but, for the most part, everyone in town seemed to be okay with Roman being around. Especially Reagan.

Her son had never been outdoors more than he was the few days before the holiday. His class trip was only two days away, but from the looks of it, he'd changed his mind and wanted to stay home to be with Roman.

She couldn't help feel a little jealous of their instant friendship, but she knew that it wasn't only good for Reagan, but Roman as well.

Jenny had come through for her and that morning there were two charter boats sitting docked outside, both of them booked for the rest of the weekend. Marv was working the ferry for the day, which meant Roman and Reagan were helping her out in the store, which would close early so they could head to the beach and watch the fireworks as a family.

It was busy in the store and, for the most part,

the day flew by since. Roman had taken charge of Reagan that day and they were out somewhere together. She still worried, even though she completely trusted Roman. She'd always known he'd be a great father.

He'd filled her in on starting the Spring Haven Home for children and Paradise Construction with Marcus. She had a million questions about his businesses and he'd patiently answered all of them.

She'd been shocked to learn that he didn't really make money on either, but that he had kept his bills paid by investing in a bunch of other businesses around their hometown.

In the few days he'd been around, she could tell he had a knack for running a business, something she had found out a few years ago that she enjoyed as well. She wondered if that was something they had always had in common.

Roman and Reagan waltzed back into the store just as the sun was setting and she was closing up.

"Ready?" Roman asked. She could tell from their faces that something was up.

"Yes." She looked between the pair and then put her hands on her hips. "What's up with you two?"

The two looked at one another and shook their heads. "We're just happy that we get to see the fireworks with you," Reagan added, his eyes sparkling.

"Right." She shook her head. "Fine, if you don't

want to tell me…" She shrugged her shoulders. "Then I may not share what's in here." She bent down and pulled out a large picnic basket.

She could tell her son was about to cave, but then Roman put his hands on his shoulders. "We have a surprise for you. Don't we, buddy?" He looked down at Reagan, who quickly nodded his head and closed his lips.

"Is that all I'm getting?" She waited and when they both nodded in unison, she sighed. "Fine, then I guess it depends on how much I like the surprise if I'm going to share this." She patted the basket.

Chapter Thirteen

Roman and Reagan stood back and watched the surprised look on Missy's face and smiled. At first she frowned when they stopped in front of the yellow sailboat, then she laughed and smiled down at the small boat.

"You rented this?" she asked.

He just smiled and said, "We thought you'd like to watch the fireworks from the water."

She reached down and hugged Reagan, then looked up at Roman. "Thank you, it's perfect. I suppose…"—she looked down at the boy—"that I'll be sharing my basket after all."

Reagan cheered as he jumped into the boat.

They'd both enjoyed sailing as kids on the Grayton's old boat and had spent countless summer days and nights on the water.

Missy settled easily on the cushions as he steered the small boat out of the harbor. Reagan helped him steer by standing in front of him.

"I've never steered a sail boat before." Reagan sounded excited.

"It's just like the ferry." Roman glanced down at Missy, who raised her eyebrows. "Which he hasn't done more than once," he added, and she smiled. "We'll just head over to that little cove area." He pointed down the shore a ways. "Think you can get us there, Captain Reagan?"

"Sure thing, first mate," Reagan said in his best pirate voice.

Roman chuckled then moved over to sit next to Missy. When he wrapped his arm around her, she settled closer to him.

"Thank you." She glanced up at him.

"For?" He waited.

"This." She nodded to the boat. "I didn't realize how much I'd missed being on the water like this."

He pulled her closer. "You know, I fixed up Julie's old sailboat."

"Oh?" She smiled. "I bet she really enjoys it now."

He nodded. "Of course, we still head out on it

each year to Crab Island to watch the fireworks." He sighed, missing his family.

"Roman." She pulled away. "You could always…"

He stopped her by shaking his head. "I'm here where I want to be. With our family." He leaned down and kissed her.

They settled the small boat and Missy pulled out the food from the basket and they enjoyed chicken, mashed potatoes, beans, and even some carrot cake that Jenny had made.

They finished up just in time for the first fireworks to go off. Reagan sat on his lap and oohed and ahhed with each bang. He pulled Missy closer and had never felt more right than he did at that moment.

When Reagan started to fall asleep after the fireworks were all over, Missy carried him below and laid him on the queen-size bed. When she came back up, she was carrying a cold beer for him.

"My kind of woman." He chuckled as he took a sip and then handed it back to her. She took a deep drink from it and sighed.

"I've been thinking about getting one of these and renting them out. That way, if I want to go out on the water anytime, I could."

He nodded. "Solid business plan. That's why I went ahead and bought this beauty today."

"What?" She leaned back, frowning up at him. "You bought this boat?"

He chuckled. "It seemed easier than renting one. Do you know how much they wanted for just a few hours aboard?"

"No, how much?" She leaned in closer, causing his body to react. "Oh, no. No business talk tonight. We can go over my smart move tomorrow during business hours." He pulled her close again and ran his lips over hers.

"This is really nice," she said as she sighed and held onto him. "A perfect night."

He nodded in agreement. "What would make it even better is taking a dip with me." He nodded to the water. "Or are you still afraid of the water after dark?"

She chuckled. "There are a lot more fish in there after dark than in the sunlight."

He laughed. "Are you even listening to what you're saying?" He smiled.

"You know what I mean. During the day, I can see them." She cringed. "Besides, after all the stories you boys told Cass and I…" He watched the sadness flood her eyes when she mentioned their sister. Then she shook her head and smiled at him. "It's no wonder I have a phobia."

He stood up and took her hand, then pulled her up next to him. "Well, since I'd like to make love to you and can't do so with a sleeping eight-year-old just a few feet away, I guess we'd better head back in."

She sighed and wrapped her arms around him. "Maybe I can bear a quick dip." She leaned up and kissed him.

He chuckled and then moaned a little as she stood back and pulled her top over her head. She was wearing a white bikini top, which caused his mouth to water. He watched her slow movements as she removed her shorts to a matching pair of bikini bottoms. He felt himself grow unbearably hard in just a few seconds.

When she walked back to him, her fingers tugging lightly on his shirt, he helped her remove his top and followed her down the ladder into the warm, dark water.

Since they had weighed anchor in the cove, they could both easily touch the sandy bottom.

"Shuffle your feet," she said as she moved farther away from the boat. "We have skates here."

He sighed. He hated the little buggers. They looked like rays but sent a nasty shock up your leg when you stepped on them. Some even bit. Shuffling his feet, he followed her until they were only knee deep. The moon was almost full, and since there wasn't a cloud in the sky, they could both see the sandy beach area.

He took her hand as he glanced back at the boat, which was only about twenty feet away. "Will he be okay?"

She nodded. "If he wakes up, we'll hear him." She pulled him farther onto the shore. "Now, you mentioned something about making love?"

He pulled her close and covered her lips with his. Her swimsuit was easy to pull off, and soon she lay under him in the sand, beautifully naked for him to enjoy. He ran his hands and mouth over her, tasting the salty water on her skin.

When he slid into her, he told her exactly how he felt about her. He felt her tense, so he quickly covered her lips and ran his tongue over hers. When he heard her moan with pleasure, he followed her and told her once more.

"Get used to hearing it," he said just below her ear as their skin cooled off from the intense pleasure. "I've only been in love with one woman my entire life." He leaned up and looked down at her, waiting until her eyes fell on his. "There's no escaping how I feel about you."

***

"There's no escaping how I feel about you." Roman's words played over in her head for the next few days. Even when she kissed Reagan goodbye and watched him load onto the bus that would take him and his classmates to Orlando, she couldn't get it off of her mind.

She knew in her heart that she loved Roman. Always had. Just like him, she'd only loved one man her entire life. Him. But even now, she knew that it wasn't possible for them to be together. Not like they wanted.

There were too many obstacles for them to jump. Too many dangers lurking just around the corner.

The first night Reagan was gone, Roman cooked her chicken cashew salad and made love to her on the kitchen countertop. The second night, after ordering Chinese takeout, he made love to her on the sofa. The third, they'd made love in the back seat of her car after he'd taken her out for Italian and parked on the beach to watch the sunset.

Every night, he consumed her mind and body so that she never really had time to feel the empty spot where their son was. Each day he told her that he loved her. Each time it shocked her system to the core. They still hadn't talked much about it. She guessed that he was just trying to get her used to hearing those words from him.

Roman brought her a large bundle of wild flowers and delivered them to the store. They had even dressed up one night and gone to the local steak house and had a fancy dinner with champagne. She'd never been treated so wonderfully before.

Every day, Reagan texted them pictures of his trip and told them how much fun he was having, but if it hadn't been for Roman, she would have gone a little mad. The morning before Reagan was set to return, they drove down to Apalachicola for some of the best blueberry pancakes she'd ever had.

The rest of the day seemed to be one of the slowest ever. Since the holiday rush was over, the slowness of the store caused her to sit and stare out the window for hours in between customers.

Roman was working the ferry that day so even he couldn't help pass the time. Minutes seemed like hours as she waited to see the bus drive by the store. She'd never been away from Reagan so long. It was still two hours before the bus was due to arrive and she was going crazy.

"Why don't you go out with the next ferry and keep Roman company?" Jenny asked, leaning on the counter.

She sighed and looked at her friend. "Is it that obvious?"

Jenny laughed. "You're driving me nuts."

"Fine, I guess it couldn't hurt. Besides, it's dead around here anyway."

"I made some brownies last night." Jenny nodded to a plate under the counter. "I bet Roman would like some."

She smiled and took the plate. "We should sell these."

Jenny's eyebrows went up. "I'm not that into baking to keep up with the demand." She smiled. "Besides, I only bake for friends."

“The whole town is your friend.” Missy laughed as she jogged out the door to catch the ferry.

“Hey, this is a nice surprise,” Roman said as she walked in.

“I brought brownies.” She smiled. “I bothered Jenny enough that she gave us the entire plate.” She held them up and wiggled her eyebrows.

Roman laughed. “Can the day go any slower?” he asked when she sat next to him.

“Sheesh! I know.” She rolled her eyes. “I can’t believe it.”

He chuckled and pulled her close for just a moment. “We’ll make the last two hours go by faster.” She smiled and hugged him.

***

Cole glanced down at the red dot on his phone and cursed. He’d been sitting outside of the small house for almost an hour. Still, when he rang the door, no one answered, least of all his brother.

The most he could tell was that the place was well kept. The metal roof looked fairly new and the siding was freshly painted a light teal. Even the white picket fence out front was spotless. He wondered whose house it was, and why his brother’s cell phone would be left there, unattended.

Roman never went anywhere without his phone.

Then he remembered the day his brother had left and felt a sick feeling wash over him, causing him to curse once more.

Just then, a dark-haired kid rode his bike up to the house. When the kid dumped his bike in the front yard, Cole jumped from the truck and rushed over.

"Hey," he called out, and the boy turned around quickly and glared at him.

"Hey," he finally said when he realized Cole wasn't going to cross the fence line.

"Do you know Roman Grayton?" he called out.

The kid squinted his eyes at him, and Cole felt a wave of deja vu hit him. Then the kid put his hand up and blocked out the sun. "Yeah."

Cole sighed. "Is he staying here?"

The kid shrugged his shoulders. "Maybe. Why?"

"He's my brother and I'm looking for him."

"He's down at the docks," the kid said, and then he turned to go into the house.

"Which docks?" he called out, but the kid was already inside. Cole smiled when he heard the locks click behind him. Smart kid.

The docks were less than three blocks away, but he drove since he didn't know exactly where he'd end up. He spotted his brother's car right away, since there were only two large buildings along the road.

Pulling in next to Roman's car, he sighed and looked at the sign above the door.

"Dog's Landing" was etched in thick wood and painted a bright teal. The shop looked like a free-for-all type of store, not unlike many he'd seen in his life.

When he walked in, he realized it wasn't actually like any he'd seen before. While most shops like this were cluttered and unorganized, this one was spotless. Its narrow aisles were neatly filled with groceries, gifts, and everything one would need on a vacation stay in the area, including bait and fishing tackle.

Walking up to the counter, he smiled at the pretty brunette behind the counter.

"Can I help you?"

"I hope so…"—he glanced at her name tag—"Jenny. I'm looking for my brother, Roman."

She smiled and nodded. "He's helping Missy out on the boats today." Cole felt his fingers start to tingle.

"Missy? Marissa?" His voice sounded hollow.

When Jenny nodded, he felt a wave of relief rush through him, followed quickly by anger. "Where can I find him?" he asked between clenched teeth.

Jenny blinked and looked around. "Um, the

boat should be coming back"—she looked down at her watch—"in about ten minutes."

He nodded and left the store without another word. He stepped out on the large deck of the pier, reached in his pocket for his phone, and dialed Marcus.

"Hey." Hearing his brother's voice helped calm him a little.

"You'll never believe where I am."

"Aren't you back from Hawaii yet?"

"Yes, I'm in Carrabelle, chasing down our crazy brother, who appears to have found Marissa."

"What?" Cole could hear he had his brother's full attention. "Have you seen her?"

"No, not yet." The phone was silent for a while.

"Maybe you should come back."

"What?" Cole blinked a few times.

"Listen, if Roman hasn't called to tell us that he's found Marissa, maybe he has a good reason."

Cole shook his head, not sure if he was hearing Marcus right. "Are you nuts?"

"Maybe he's trying to convince her not to get spooked away again."

He thought about it and felt his heart skip. Damn, why hadn't he thought of it. Marissa might still be running from whatever had caused her to leave all those years ago, and if anyone could convince her to come back, it was Roman.

He'd called his brother a few times and he'd had been very vague with what he'd told him, never once mentioning where he was or what he was doing.

Chapter Fourteen

When Roman and Missy drove up to the house, they were both a little shocked to see Reagan's bike laying in the front yard. He had gotten home early and they rushed in the front door and both of them engulfed him in a hug until the boy started complaining.

"What do you say we go have some pizza and you tell us all about your trip?" Missy suggested.

"Augh." Reagan surprised them by rolling his eyes. "I'm kind of pizza'd out. How about a burger at Bayside?"

Roman smiled and nodded. “I could use a burger. If we can drive your car.” He smiled when she nodded. Her narrow driveway could only fit one car at a time, so he quickly backed his sedan up and parked it on the street then pulled out the classic and waited while Missy and Reagan loaded up.

“Oh,” Reagan said as he pulled out of the driveway. “Your brother came by today.”

Roman slammed on the breaks a little too quickly. “My…” He turned and looked at Reagan, then glanced at Missy, who had turned pale. “What did he look like? When?” He shook his head.

“He was here, sitting in an old truck when I got home.” Reagan shrugged his shoulders. “He looked like a surfer. You know, Mom, the one we saw on that ad in your magazine.”

Roman turned to Missy. “I don’t know how he found me. I haven’t told him anything.”

He watched her close her eyes and sigh. “It was bound to happen, sooner or later.” When she looked at him again, he could see the fear in her eyes.

“He must have Lo-jacked my phone.” He chuckled. “You know how he is.” He brushed a hand down her shoulder. When she jumped, he pulled the car into park and pulled her closer. “Missy, I swear, you’re still safe here.”

“Why wouldn’t she be? Is your brother a bad guy?” Reagan asked from the back seat.

"Oh." Missy covered her mouth with her hand and spun around. "No, honey. Cole is wonderful. He's…." She looked at Roman for a moment. "He's our relative." She sighed. "Maybe we can tell you the story over a burger?" she asked after hearing Roman's stomach growl loudly. He shrugged his shoulders.

"The brownies were my lunch," he said.

Missy smiled. He could see that the smile didn't reach her eyes and feared that she was once more thinking of running. Even with everything she'd built here, he knew she wouldn't hesitate to pick up and leave if it meant keeping Reagan safe.

He drove slowly towards Bayside Burgers down the coastal highway, enjoying the warm air coming off the Gulf. He'd flipped on the radio to the oldies station, which only seemed natural in a classic car.

When the news bulletin came on mentioning something about a hurricane, he pulled over and turned it up so they could listen.

"Gulf coast states are preparing to be hit by Tropical Storm Donna, which is set to make landfall between Southeastern Louisiana and the Florida Panhandle around midday Thursday. The National Hurricane Center has issued warnings stretching from…"

He reached over and turned the radio down.

"Well?" He turned to Missy. "What is your plan for hurricanes?"

She chuckled. "Tie everything down and wait them out. Half of the time it's not nearly as bad as they've predicted." She shrugged. "We've waited out a few since being here." She glanced at Reagan and smiled. "Now we've got the new roof and clean gutters." She looked at him and nodded. "Thanks to you, the house should be ready."

He could tell she was nervous and knew she wanted to say more, but not in front of Reagan. Pulling the car back onto the highway, he drove faster to the burger joint.

When they got there, he pulled Missy aside. "I'll be right in. I have a…. call to make." She frowned but nodded then went in the diner with Reagan.

Pulling out his phone, he decided to send a text to Cole instead since he didn't feel like arguing with his brother at the moment.

-Heard you stopped by. Thanks for not sticking around. Give her some time. She's warming up to the idea of coming home soon. R

When he walked in, he slid into the booth next to Missy and glanced down at the menu, not really feeling hungry anymore. Still, he ordered a burger and waited for her to make the next move.

Finally, after a few minutes of silence, she leaned forward and took Reagan's hand. "Cole is my brother." She sighed. "My adopted brother. I have three adopted brothers and one sister." She looked to him for just a moment. "Roman is one of them as well."

"But," Reagan said, shaking his head, sending his dark hair flying. "If you two are brother and sister…"

"Adopted. Your mother came into the family when she was… your age." He looked at her and smiled when she nodded. "I was almost a year older." He smiled and reached across the table to take the kid's other hand. "We had both come from bad situations." He looked to her to take over.

"I was raised by some pretty crazy people." She closed her eyes for a brief moment. "This wonderful woman, an angel really—her name was Lilly—she helped me escape the prison I had been born and raised in and brought me to live with the Graytons." She nodded to Roman. "I lived there until someone tracked me down and threatened me. Then I ran away." She looked off, out towards the window.

"What about you?" Reagan turned to him after a moment of silence.

"Me?" He blinked and dropped the kid's hand.

"Sure, did Lilly help you escape too?"

He sighed. "No, not really. Yes, she was the one who brought me to live with my new family."

"Did you escape a prison, too?" he asked.

Shaking his head, he reached over and took Missy's hand in his. He wouldn't have the power to recount his story without feeling her strength.

"I had a different kind of prison. My real father"—he swallowed the foul taste in his mouth that always came with the thought of the evil man —"was a boxer. He was the kind of man that took his anger out on his son all the time. When I was seven, my father lost a match and when he got home, decided to take his frustration out on me. I ended up in the hospital for two weeks. Then Lilly came and took me away." He hadn't realized tears were streaming down his face until Missy reached over and wiped them away gently with her fingers.

"Roman's the one that taught me how to box in junior high. There was a group of girls that were dead set on picking on me." She smiled at him. "Then, in gym class one day, I showed them what I could do with the punching bag and they never bothered me again." She squeezed his hand.

Roman turned to Reagan. "That's why I started Spring Haven Home for kids, where we grew up. I wanted to help other kids who had come from bad situations."

Reagan leaned forward. "What do you do there?"

"We help kids, give them everything they need. A place to stay until they can find a new family, teaching them to read and write." He looked to Missy and smiled. "Teaching them to defend themselves."

"Can I come and see it sometime?" Reagan

asked.

Roman's smile fell away and he felt his heart jump. Then he looked over at Missy. "If it's okay with your mother."

***

Missy felt tears build up behind her eyes and had to look out the window once more. She was saved from answering when their burgers arrived. She could hardly swallow a bite of her meal through the lump in her throat.

She wanted more than anything to go home. To allow Reagan to know her family. To visit Roman's home for kids. But she knew the risks. She'd been locked in the compound more than once and knew what would happen if they ever got their hands on Reagan.

History was full of psycho religious cults; lives lost, families separated, children being sacrificed. No, she'd come too far to protect herself and Reagan against this.

As they drove the stretch of road back to her small home, she began to organize a plan in her mind. Pain stabbed at her heart when she thought about leaving Carrabelle, but at this point, it was the only way to protect her son.

The next day, she started bright and early. Before Roman was up, she had packed two bags and hidden them in the trunk of her car.

They were busy preparing the store for the

upcoming storm, but during her break, she drove to the bank and pulled out all of her money and shoved it in the trunk of the car in a bag. It wasn't much, since most of what she had had been put back into the store.

Just the thought of leaving everything she'd built had her heart breaking a little more, but fear was overwhelming.

They had spent the evening at home, locking everything down for the storm that was set to hit them the next day.

As she lay in bed with Roman that night, she knew it would be their last together. She'd tried to fool herself into thinking it could work out with him—living here, hiding from her family, both of them. But, if Cole could find them so easily—she closed her mind to the thought of what else could happen.

Rolling over, she decided to make the most of her last night with him. When she started kissing him, his hands moved up into her hair, pulling her closer. She trailed her fingers over his chest, enjoying the play of muscles and taut skin.

Her legs held him down, pinned to the bed, as she ran her mouth down over his chest where her fingers had just been. His fingers dug into her shoulders, holding her to him. She smiled when she heard him groan her name.

When she gently pulled his shorts down his hips, he cupped her elbows and brought her back up to him. Then he was rolling and pinning her to the bed.

"What do you think you're doing?" He almost growled it.

For a moment, her heart refused to beat. Then he smiled down at her. "You're torture won't work on me tonight."

She released the breath she'd been holding. Then he was kissing her, causing her breath to hitch for different reasons. He gently removed her nightshirt and then her sleeping shorts. When she lay underneath him totally naked, he pulled back and looked down at her.

She sat up and took his face in her hands, kissing him like it was her last time. She poured every ounce of emotion into the kiss. Her skin heated next to his and she pulled him closer until, finally, he filled her completely. Dual moans echoed in the room as their bodies moved against one another.

Finally, she threw her head back and felt herself slide. He stiffened above her and she opened her eyes to watch him in pure delight.

When he lay down beside her, his fingers running over her skin, he whispered, "Beautiful." Then he broke her heart further by saying, "I love you." He looked deep into her eyes and said it again.

Tears streamed down her face and when he

leaned closer to wipe them away, she took his face in her hands and whispered, “I love you too. I always have. I always will.”

Chapter Fifteen

The rain started early that next morning. Roman stood outside on the front porch, drinking his coffee and watching the sky grow darker. Missy's words played over and over again in his mind. She'd told him that she'd loved him. Always had. He'd never been happier than at that moment.

He heard the front door open and close and turned as Missy stepped out, fully dressed.

"Going somewhere?" He'd yet to pull on anything more than shorts and a T-shirt.

She nodded. "I'm going to take Reagan really quick to the shop. I want to get a few more things before the storm hits."

He smiled. "I can do that." He pulled her closer, feeling her tense slightly.

"No." She shook her head. "I promised him I'd take him." She smiled and then leaned down and kissed him until he forgot what they'd been talking about. "It shouldn't take too long." She smiled and then turned away.

"The storm's set to hit in a few hours," he called after her. She nodded and waved as she walked down the walkway towards her car. His was still parked in the street from the other night. He watched the pair drive away and waved as they headed towards the store.

He'd spent many hours waiting out a hurricane since living along the coast. Most were just tropical storms, but some had been pretty bad. Donna had not progressed to something locals feared. At least not yet. If he'd learned one thing living along the coast, it was to always be prepared.

Walking inside, he locked the front door and made sure everything was far from the windows. He changed his clothes and then walked around the outside of the house, shielding himself from the wind and rain with an umbrella.

An hour later, Missy and Reagan had yet to return, and he was starting to freak out. Pulling his keys out, he jumped in his car and drove the few blocks to the store. When he saw her car parked out front, he sighed with relief.

However, when he entered the store, he quickly realized that they weren't there. He rushed around the small place, calling their names over and over again.

Just as he was about to call the police, Missy rushed in the front door, soaking wet.

"I can't find Reagan!" Tears were streaming down her face as her breath hitched out.

"What?" He rushed to her, taking her shoulders into his hands. She was freezing cold to the touch. "What happened?" he asked, pulling her closer.

"I…" She cried into his chest. "He's mad at me and he ran off."

"What?" He pulled her back, looking into her eyes. "Why is he mad?"

"I…" She closed her eyes. "I told him that we are leaving."

He felt his fingers tighten on her shoulders. "Going where?" he said with clenched teeth. He knew the answer wasn't Spring Haven when she looked up at him. "You're running again?" he growled out.

She looked down at her feet and nodded. "It's the only way I can keep him safe." Her eyes moved back up to his, begging him to understand.

"Where did he go?"

She shivered. "I didn't see. I was packing up some stuff that we'd need." She nodded to two large boxes full of food, clothing, and items. "He asked what I was doing. Before I knew it, he was gone." She looked around. "I've looked everywhere."

"How long ago did he go?" he asked, rushing over and yanking off his soaked jacket and pulling a heavier raincoat off the hook. He slipped on his boots and grabbed a flashlight from behind the counter.

Missy was looking at the clock on the way. "Half an hour?" She looked at him, feeling the need to explain. "Roman…"

"Save it," he growled. "I'll find him. Stay here." He glared at her then rushed out into the storm to find his son.

***

Missy paced in the store for almost an hour. When the worst part of the storm was wailing outside, she picked up the shop phone and called the police, who informed her that they had patrols out and would look for the pair. Less than half an hour later, a patrol car stopped by.

When she let Kim, the only female officer in town, in the store, she realized just how bad the storm had grown outside.

"It's getting bad out there," she said, biting her bottom lip.

"I'm sure Mr. Grayton and Reagan have taken shelter from the storm. We lost the power lines a few minutes ago," Kim said, wiping her feet. "The chief wants me to hang around here, in case they come back. He's pulled all the units from the streets." She shook her head, sending water dropping from her dark hair.

"I'm surprised you still have—" A large bolt of lightning hit and the room went dark. "Power," she said, frowning. "Sorry, guess I jinxed you."

Missy wrapped her arms around herself. "It was bound to happen." She walked back to the counter where her camping lamps sat, ready for the storm. She'd tugged off her wet clothes and had pulled on new one's she kept stocked on the shelves. The large hoodie was a few sizes too big, but she had needed the warmth. Her shoes were still soaking wet, but she didn't mind.

Several times, she'd thought about heading out in the storm, continuing her search, but something had told her to stay put.

Less than an hour later, when the storm had died down a little, Jenny showed up with her grandfather. Bob came a few minutes later.

"We heard. What can we do to help?" John asked.

Her eyes stung as more and more of the townspeople she'd come to know flooded into the small store. Apparently, as they had looked, the police had spread the word that Roman and Reagan were missing.

Someone was always with her, as townspeople flooded the streets of Carrabelle, looking for her family. A hot cup of tea was always kept in front of her, along with Jenny's hurricane cookies and desserts.

She couldn't even swallow a bite or sip. Instead, she worried constantly.

By that evening, the storm was pretty much over and still no one had seen or heard from Roman or Reagan. Missy had worried herself into such a state that no matter what anyone said to her, she was sure that they were both dead somewhere.

Walking over to where Roman hung his jacket, she pulled it on and closed her eyes when his scent hit her. She'd been such a fool. Had she really believed that running away would solve anything? Especially after she'd finally admitted that she'd been in love with him her entire life.

When her hands dropped down, she banged something solid and slowly pulled out his cell phone.

When she turned it on, she flipped through the numbers and when she saw Marcus' name, she hit dial without thinking.

"Yo," the familiar voice said in her ear, causing her breath to hitch.

"Marcus?" It came out as a whisper.

She could hear loud voices and a bunch of noises. She heard him moving around, and then the line was silent for a while.

"Marissa? Is that you?" She heard his voice hitch.

Nodding, she wiped the tears from her eyes. "Yes," she sighed.

"My god." She heard the emotions in his voice. "I never thought he'd do it." Then he laughed. "Tell that brother of ours—"

"He's missing," she broke in as her voice hitched. "I… we can't find him. He went to look for Reagan, but they never came back." She continued with the entire story quickly. She had to lean against the wall since she'd become light-headed.

"Where are you? Carrabelle?" he asked once she was done, which only reassured her that her family already knew where she was.

She nodded again. "Yes."

"We'll be there shortly." She heard him moving around. "Missy, don't go anywhere again." She heard the begging in his voice and could only nod once more as he hung up.

***

Marcus walked into Wendy's hospital room and coughed lightly when he saw Cole leaning over the blonde bartender, kissing her like there was no tomorrow.

"Sorry, Cole, I need to borrow you for a

moment," he said in a strained tone.

Cole stood up and reached for Wendy's hand. "I'll be right back." He leaned in and kissed her once more.

"What is it?" Cole asked the second he stepped out into the hallway.

"Roman and the kid are gone."

"What?" Cole gripped his arm like he needed the extra strength.

He nodded. "I guess she was going to take off again, but the kid beat her to it. Roman went to look for him just before the storm hit." He shook his head. "They've had the police and the entire town looking for them and have come up empty-handed."

Cole nodded. "Get as many guys as you can. I'll be right out." He watched his brother walk back into Wendy's hospital room.

Marcus turned back to the waiting room where Shelly, Marcus's fiancee, Cassey, Luke, and Wendy's sister, Willow, were sitting all hunched together.

"Luke, you're with me." He nodded as he started walking out.

"Wait!" Cassey stood, her hands going to her hips. "Where in heck do you think you're taking my husband?"

He turned to her, his eyes full of sadness. He'd

hoped he could escape without telling her, but he should have known better.

"Marcus." Shelly walked over to him, her arms wrapping around his waist. "What's wrong?" He should have known that he couldn't have hidden anything from his fiancée, the mother of his child. He smiled down at her at that thought. Putting a protective hand over their growing child, he looked over to his sister.

"To find Roman."

"What's happened?" Cassey rushed over to him.

"He's missing." He hoped she would end the questions there, but she just crossed her arms over her chest as Cole rushed out.

"Where does Missy say she saw them last?" his brother blurted out. Marcus' eyes moved to Cassey, who had turned very pale. Luke noticed and rushed to his wife's side.

"Missy?" Her voice was very soft as her eyes bore into his.

He nodded. "Roman found her in Carrabelle. She has a son. The kid took off before the storm, and Roman went to look for him. Now they're both missing."

Cassey wrapped her arms around Luke as tears streamed down her face. Then she shocked him by pulling back and exclaiming in a loud voice, "I'm going with you."

Marcus drove, since Cole looked too tired and worn out from his excursion in the wild surf and his whole ordeal with Wendy being hurt. Luke sat in the back seat of the truck, holding Cassey as she glanced out the window silently.

When they arrived in town, which appeared to have been hit harder than Surf Breeze had, it was shortly after dark. They drove up to the small store, Dog's Landing, which Cole had directed them to. There were two police cars in the parking lot.

When they walked in the store, the three of them stood there, looking at their long-lost sister.

***

Missy heard and saw the lights from the car when it drove in. Her breath stilled at the thought that she would be coming face-to-face with one of her family members. She stood up and walked towards the doors, waiting.

Instead of one of her brothers, she was shocked to see her entire family walk in. Her eyes ran over her brother's and Cassey's faces. So much had changed in each of them, but still, she would have recognized them anywhere.

She didn't know what to do, so she stood there, hugging her arms tightly around herself until Cassey finally cried out and rushed to her, wrapping her arms around her shoulders and pulling her close.

Tears streamed from her eyes as her sister held

onto her tightly. Then she felt Cole and Marcus join in and she completely lost it and cried until her head hurt and she'd gone blind with tears.

Someone in the room cleared their throat, breaking the spell. Marcus and Cole pulled back, wiping their eyes quickly. Cassey still held onto her with one arm wrapped around her shoulders.

"Tell us everything and do it quickly so we can get out there and look for them," Marcus said.

She repeated her story, leaving out the part about how she had been determined to leave a second time. She told them that Reagan was Roman's son, not looking one of them in the eyes the entire time she spoke. She was handed another cup of hot tea, and had taken several sips when her throat closed up.

"Do you have any clue where they might have gone?" Cassey asked, taking her hand in hers.

She shook her head. "They've checked my house and the boats are all still here. Even the sailboat." She closed her eyes feeling the sinking feeling again in her chest.

She watched as Marcus, Cole, and Cassey's husband, Luke, disappeared out the front door of the store to join the search.

"There's so much destruction out there." She nodded towards the door.

"This place doesn't look like it got hit too bad." Cassey smiled.

She nodded. “I’m thankful, but still, they could be trapped…”

“Don’t think about it. If I know Roman, he’d do everything in his power to protect your son.”

Missy sighed and looked over at her sister. “I’m sorry.”

Cassey’s eyes teared up again.

“I was young and stupid. Most of all, I was scared.”

“Of?” Cassey blinked a few times. “Of us?”

Missy shook her head. “No, of my family.” She sighed and settled back to tell her sister the entire story.

By the time she’d run through everything, her head was throbbing. Walking over, she grabbed a bottle of aspirin and swallowed two pills with her warm tea.

“Here, have something to eat.” Cassey shoved a plate of spaghetti someone had brought for the searchers.

Shaking her head, she started to push the plate aside. “I can’t…”

“Eat. You need it.” She pulled a plate in front of herself and took a bite. “See, it’s good.”

Missy laughed. “Fine.” She sat next to Cassey and took a few bites.

When the front door chimed, they both rushed

out of the back room.

Marcus, Cole, and Luke walked in with two deputies. "Sorry, we're just dropping Cole off." Marcus nodded to his brother. Cole looked like death.

"Are you okay?" Missy rushed to his side.

He nodded. "Yeah, just wiped." He ran a hand through his hair.

"Wiped and worried about Wendy," Luke said, helping his brother-in-law to sit.

"Sorry," Cole said, looking into Missy's eyes.

"It's okay." She smiled at him. "Rest a while."

"I'd like to get back to Wendy. Then maybe in the morning I can come back."

She nodded. "Is Wendy…?"

He smiled slightly. "My fiancée." Then he frowned. "She was hit in the head with some debris."

Worry instantly flooded Missy's mind. Hadn't she thought that about Roman and Reagan since the moment they'd walked out the door?

"Hey," Cole said softly, "I'm sure they're okay. Wendy just has a conk on the head. She's okay and our brother and your son will be too."

She nodded, swallowing her worry.

"I can take you back to the hospital," one of the

officers said. "I'm off duty and I wanted to check in on my folks who live near there."

Cole nodded. "I'd appreciate it." He looked towards Marcus. "Keep me posted."

After Cole left, the rest of the crew disappeared back into the darkness. Missy and Cassey waited along with Jenny and a few other people. They had set up cots in the back room and they were taking shifts napping. She'd even tried to catch a few minutes, but her mind kept whirling, not allowing her to sleep.

By mid-morning, Cole had joined the search again.

In their search, they had helped several families trapped in the rubble that used to be their homes. As the day passed, more and more people crowded the store. She'd opened it up and had fed everyone with items on her shelves and had given some in need new clothes as well.

The Red Cross had arrived early that morning and had set up in her parking lot. She walked around like she was in a trance until that evening when Marcus walked back in with the police chief on his heels.

"Missy," he said, looking towards Cassey, who hadn't left her side the entire time. "We just ran into Mrs. Miller at the school. As you know, she lives across the street from the school." He walked over to her and leaned down. "She claims she saw Reagan sitting outside on the playground in the rain, and when she went out to get him, she noticed that Roman was already there, talking to him. This was just before the storm hit."

Missy's heart skipped and she felt her breath hitch. "Are they…"

Marcus shook his head. "We've searched the entire school grounds. It's empty. But she does remember a strange van in the parking lot as they started to leave. She was busy trying to make sure her house was secure, and by the time she turned around, Roman and Reagan were gone. So was the van."

Missy's head spun as realization dawn. "My father," she said, just before everything went black.

Chapter Sixteen

Roman held his head up and groaned with pain. Blood was dripping down the side of his face, getting into his eyes. He felt Reagan's small body next to his and when he reached out to pull him close, he realized his hands were tied tightly behind his back.

When he opened his eyes, it was pitch dark. He could hear that the storm was in full force outside the vehicle, but it was too dark inside to see clearly. He could tell they were driving slowly, since the van kept swaying with the wind. From the sound of it, they were traveling less than twenty miles per hour.

There were no windows in the back of the van

and when he kicked out, he hit someone, who grunted.

"He's awake," the man said.

"Don't worry, he's tied up," a deep voice from the front said.

"What about the boy?" the first voice asked.

"He'll be out for a while," the deeper voice said.

"Are you sure of the amount you gave him?"

"Quiet," the deeper voice growled.

"What are we to do with the man?"

"He'll pay for his crimes."

After that, it was silent.

Roman felt around with his hands, trying to see if there was anything he could use to cut his hands free. He'd removed his own jacket and was wearing the raincoat, which didn't have any pockets. He remembered his cell phone in his other jacket and almost groaned out loud.

Maybe Reagan had something in his pockets that could help him. He rolled over and started running his hands over his son.

"Easy," the person sitting next to him said. "Just stay still. This will all be over soon enough."

"Where are you taking us?" he demanded, wanting to keep the man busy while he searched Reagan's pockets.

"We're taking the boy home," the deep-voiced man answered.

"What about me?" he asked, finally feeling Reagan's house key in his jean pocket. He pulled it out and started working on the duct tape around his wrists.

"You're just in the way," the driver said.

"You're from the Council of Friends," he said, feeling the tape give a little.

"What do you know of the CoF?" the driver growled.

"Plenty." He smiled. In the time he'd been in Carrabelle, he'd done lots of research into the cult.

"I know that the branch moved to just south of Tallahassee in the early 80s. That it's run by a man named Kevin Smith, who claims he's Reagan's grandfather."

"The boy is my grandson," the deeper voice growled.

Roman chuckled. "Reagan's grandfather, Mark Grayton, will have something to say about that."

"That man has no blood hold on this boy."

"No." He finished removing the tape and took a couple deep breaths. "But he has something you'll never have."

"What?" He felt the van slow down.

"Him." He reached over and grabbed Reagan's

lax body, just as he kicked the younger man who was sitting at his feet. The man when flying backwards, giving Roman enough time to get the van door open.

He was immediately soaked from the rain and when he jumped from the van, he realized they had been going faster than he'd expected.

He hit the ground and rolled, protecting Reagan as he went flying through mud and grass. A small tree was in his way and when he hit it, bark and needles stuck in his skin.

When he finally settled, he picked himself up, holding Reagan's body close to him as he headed in the opposite direction of the van.

The men stood at the back of the van and laughed, actually laughed at him.

Taking a moment to look around, he realized why they weren't chasing him. It was too late. They were already on the CoF compound.

***

Missy woke up with several people looking down at her.

"She's awake," Cassey said, taking her hand. "Are you okay, sweetie?"

She nodded and started to sit up, then remembered why she'd passed out in the first place. "Roman, Reagan," she cried.

"If you know anything about who was in that

van, you'd better share it with us," the chief of police said. He was standing next to Marcus, looking stern.

She rubbed her hand over her forehead, fighting the pain. "The CoF has them."

"Who?" Cassey asked.

"The Council of Friends." She closed her eyes and leaned back, wishing it was all just a bad dream. "I was too late."

"Who the heck is the Council of—"

"Friends." She finished Marcus' statement. "It's a cult." She sat up and looked at her family. "The cult I was born and raised in, until I escaped and came to the Graytons."

"Why would they take Roman and your son?" Someone asked.

She shook her head. "They don't want Roman."

"Okay, why do they want your son?" Marcus asked, sounding pissed.

"Because he's the chosen one," she said, realizing how stupid it all sounded.

"What?" Cassey frowned. "What the heck is a chosen one and why do they think your son is him?"

She rolled her shoulders and started yet another story. By the time she was done, everyone was looking at her like she had grown another head.

But at least she'd gotten her point across. The CoF was dangerous. Very dangerous.

"I'll drive," Marcus said as he started walking towards the door. Her laughter stopped him.

"What?" He frowned down at her.

"One doesn't simply walk into the CoF compound."

"We do. We're family. They can't…"

"Marcus, maybe we should wait," Cole said, taking hold of his brother's arm. "I dated this girl a while back." He looked over to her. "She'd been brainwashed by a cult. She really believed that aliens were going to come down and rescue everyone in her cult on the promised day." He shook his head. "Batty."

She nodded. "They won't stop. They never will. Not until Reagan leads them into the promised land."

"What exactly does that entail?" the chief of police asked.

Her eyes met his. "Total annihilation."

***

Roman ran, even though he could see the tall fences all around the large compound. There was bound to be a way out of here. Somewhere. When he came to a fence, he turned to the right and started running the length. Rain and mud splattered him as he slid. The storm was pretty much over, but lightning still flashed every so often. He could hear people shouting as they looked for them.

Finally, he found a break in the wire. The storm had knocked down an old oak tree. Its branches hung over the barbed wire. Kneeling, he slapped Reagan's face lightly; he needed the kid to be awake in order to get over the fence.

Voices neared him so he ducked behind a large bush and held his breath until they continued on. He felt Reagan jolt in his hands and quickly covered the kid's mouth in case he woke screaming.

"Easy, it's me. We're in a bind here, kiddo," he said, when Reagan's eyes met his. He smiled when the kid nodded. "I need your help. We have to get over this fence." He leaned, showing him the fallen tree.

"It's too high," the boy said. He could tell he was holding back tears. "Did they find us?" he asked.

Roman nodded, not wanting to waste any more time on stories. "I'll help you get over the top."

"What about you?" Reagan asked.

He smiled. "I'll make it just fine. You first. We have to do this fast, though, and quietly."

When Reagan nodded, he took off the heavy raincoat and handed it to him. "Throw this over the wires, so they don't stick you." The boy nodded. "Okay, ready?"

Reagan nodded again.

They rushed over to the edge of the fence. The tree was rooted on the outside, but its branches had knocked out a good section of the upper fence. When he hoisted Reagan up, the kid tossed the jacket over the wire and grabbed hold of the branches with his hands and the fence with his feet. He slipped once, but Roman was right there to help him.

He watched as his son made his way carefully and quietly down the slippery tree. When he hit the bottom, Roman took hold of the fence and started climbing. He had one leg over the wires when he heard the shouts.

"Run!" He glanced down at Reagan, who just shook his head at him. "Now! Run!" He growled it as he jumped over the wire, not bothering with using the tree. He felt a bullet fly a few inches by his head as he fell. The branch next to him exploded and shards of wood flew into his skin.

When he hit the soft ground, his left boot stuck in the mud. Yanking his foot out of the damn thing, he reached Reagan and hoisted him up in his arms as more shots rang out. Then he started running with everything he had, praying that he would be fast enough.

Chapter Seventeen

Missy sat in the back of the fed's car. She'd been over the story three times already. Once to her family and twice to the authorities. She'd answered every question they had about the CoF.

"Mrs.…." She looked up at the passenger of the car and frowned.

"Grayton," she answered without thinking.

He nodded. "Mrs. Grayton, we need you to think if there's any more information you can give us on the CoF."

"I've told you everything I know. It's been years since I escaped." She looked out the window and felt her skin crawl. They were less than five miles from the dreaded compound. A shiver ran up her spine as they continued down the road. Her family was close behind them in their own cars. There were over a dozen dark sedans, vans, and trucks following the one she was in, all with agents, prepared for a fight.

"We've had our eye on the CoF for a few years. Ever since it was made known they'd been stockpiling weapons." He turned again and looked back at her. "You don't know anything about that?"

She shook her head no. "Last time, I was held in the hospital wing. They tied me to the bed every night and didn't let me leave my room."

"How did you escape then?" he asked.

She sighed. "My mother." She blinked, remembering the sacrifice of the crazed woman who had given birth to her. "Shortly after I'd been born, she left the CoF and got back into drugs. After the visit at the Grayton's, she'd watched me. I guess she felt guilty or something. She was still trying to get herself clean. Anyway, she broke into the compound and helped me."

"Where is she now?" he asked, writing a few things down in his notepad.

"Dead," she said, a tear slipping from her eyes.

He turned and looked at her again.

"She could never shake her addiction. I found her shortly after Reagan was born, a needle in her arm." She closed her eyes on the memory. "She went into the cult to clean her life up as a teen, but they had just added to her pain and messed her up even more." She tapped her heart and her head.

He nodded and turned back to take his notes.

When the car came to a halt, she felt her stomach sink. There, a few hundred yards in front of them, stood the gated walls she'd spent a lifetime dreading.

The large gray buildings hung in the horizon like the dark symbol of dread they were. There were over a dozen smaller buildings, all painted in the same dull shade. She'd been born in one of those buildings. The tall fences were still in place, and there was a new larger electrical gate to allow people in but never out. Not unless you were Kevin Smith or with him. No one ever left. Except her and her mother. They'd been the only two who had ever escaped those barriers. Twice.

She shivered as they opened the doors then quickly shut them again when they heard gunfire. The agents quickly jumped back in the car and drove in reverse a hundred yards back.

The next few minutes seemed to go by quickly. She was shoved into the back of a van and driven even further away from the gates. Marcus, Cole, Cassey, and Julie were all there waiting for her.

She hadn't realized how much she'd missed Julie, the woman who had been more like a mother than a sister to them all.

"What's going on?" Marcus asked.

"They were shooting at us," she said, hugging herself.

"What?" Marcus glanced back at the compound, which was almost a mile away at this point.

"What's going to happen know?" Julie asked, giving Missy a hug.

Missy shook her head. "I… I don't know."

Minutes stretched into hours as negotiation teams were sent in. A base of operations was set up in a makeshift tent. At several points, they were almost ushered off site, but each time, her family fought for their right to stay. Finally, they were given their own small waiting tent and told to stay put.

When an agent walked in, he walked right up to her.

"Mrs. Grayton," he nodded. "We've spotted the van that took your husband and son."

She didn't correct him, only nodded automatically as Cassey wrapped her arms around her.

"It's parked just inside the gates. We haven't confirmed that they are in the compound yet, but are currently trying to negotiate their release."

She nodded again.

"Has anyone talked to them yet?" Cassey asked.

He shook his head no. "Not yet. We've got all the phone lines into the compound, but they've remained silent."

"What happens now?" Missy asked, rubbing her hands up and down her arms, which seemed to grow colder the longer she waited.

"We'll continue to establish a dialog. If that doesn't work, we'll send our men in. They've made their intentions clear and after Waco, we've learned that waiting them out isn't the best plan."

She nodded, feeling more light-headed at the mention of her worst nightmare. Hadn't she always believed that her father was sending his members down the same path?

After all, she could vaguely remember some of his preaching. How the apocalypse was coming and that the chosen one would lead them to the chosen land.

She'd always been told the chosen land was beyond the gates of heaven. With her father as their prophet and her son, the chosen one, now behind the walls of the compound, she only prayed that Roman would be able to save their son.

They waited around for hours, not hearing anything more, until Cassey stood up.

"Something's burning." She sniffed the air and rushed from the tent. They all rushed out after her. They stood looking towards the compound, but nothing was visible from this far away. Their arms were all around one another as they waited.

Officers in full body gear rushed around them like they were invisible. She could hear someone shouting orders and saw a group preparing to enter the compound with a battering vehicle.

Just when they were going to turn back and go into the tent, they heard a loud pop and turned back towards the building in time to see the entire place shatter into a million fireballs.

She screamed over and over again as she fell to her knees, watching the buildings blow up, one at a time. Her family stood beside her, crying and holding onto one another as the agents all scrambled back away from the heat that they could feel from almost a mile away.

Missy's knees sank slowly into the mud as she cried into her hands. When she looked up again her vision grayed, and all she could hear was a loud buzzing sound.

Tears wracked her entire body. Every joint and muscle hurt. Her skin ached and she felt as if she'd been stung by a million bees.

Her eyes were glued to the fire until she had to blink from the brightness. The cries of her family dulled in her mind as she mourned.

Then she felt a hand on her shoulder.

***

Roman was knocked to the ground when a

bullet lodged in his shoulder. Stumbling, he lost his hold on Reagan as they rolled down the embankment and landed into the muddy banks of a stream.

"Over here," someone called. "I see them."

"Roman!" Reagan cried out. "Get up!"

Roman obeyed, pushing the pain behind him. He could only hold onto Reagan with one arm, but the kid was hanging onto him like a monkey as he ran through the shallow water.

They cleared the water and had just ducked into the trees when he heard the sound of men running through the water. They were just a few yards behind them. He had to outsmart them, since he couldn't outrun them. He was reminded of all the games of hide and seek he'd had with his brothers and sisters. Games he'd always won.

Heading in the same direction, he waited until he knew the men were in the trees and then ran in a big U shape, ducking behind a large boulder and bushes as he heard them pass their hiding spot. When everything was silent, he quietly walked back to the edge of the water and waded into the stream, this time keeping with the current until he found another spot to climb out on the opposite bank.

"Do you think we lost them?" Reagan asked quietly.

He nodded and shushed his son. "We have to be

very quiet for a while." Reagan nodded as they continued to walk slowly through the brush.

When they came to a clearing, he glanced around and noticed a small pump house.

"Can we hide in there?" Reagan asked.

"No, buddy. That's the first place they'll look." He frowned. "But, maybe we can slow them down for a while. I need to set you down for a minute."

Reagan nodded. "You're bleeding." He pointed to his shoulder.

"Yeah." He frowned. "I'll need to borrow your jacket." Reagan removed his light jacket without hesitation. "Thanks, son." Roman smiled down at him. Reagan smiled back up at him.

"How can we slow them down?"

"By making them think we're hiding in there." He nodded to the pump house.

They walked closer to the small building. Roman used his clean hand and smeared some of his blood on the edge of the door. Then he used his only booted foot to kick the door in until it hung on its hinges. "Okay, we need to run now." He looked over at his son as he wrapped the boy's jacket around his shoulder to stifle the bleeding. Do you think you can run or do I need to carry you?"

"I can do it. I'm the fastest boy in my gym class."

His eyebrows shot up. "Fastest boy?"

Reagan sighed and looked down. "Susie Morgan is almost a minute faster than me."

Roman stopped himself from laughing. "Your mother could always outrun me." He smiled and wiped some dirt from Reagan's chin. "Okay, let's see how fast we can make it to those trees."

Reagan glanced up and nodded. When they took off, he had to slow his pace just to make sure the kid stayed right beside him.

They were a few yards into the trees when he heard more gunfire. This time, it was coming from the west. Back where he imagined the compound was. Taking a chance, he grabbed Reagan's hand and started running towards the sounds instead of away.

They heard the loud explosions just before exiting the trees. Then they stopped long enough to take stock of what was happening. Over six dozen vehicles were parked alongside the road. There were barriers blocking traffic and men in dark uniforms stood around.

When he took Reagan's hand this time, the kid smiled. "It's the Cavalry," the boy said, causing him to laugh.

"Even better. It's the FBI." He stepped out into the clearing, only to have several agents draw their weapons and point them directly at his chest.

"Easy." He nodded to the kid. "I think you're

here for us."

***

Missy closed her eyes and held her breath. When she turned her head, her eyes refused to open. Then soft lips settled over hers and she melted into Roman's arms.

Her arms wrapped around his shoulders as she cried and pressed her lips against his.

"Mom!" Reagan called out. Her eyes flew open as her son flung himself towards them.

She held onto them both as their family cried around them. Roman was on his knees in front of her, holding her tight.

"Sir, we need to see to those wounds," someone said over them. Gasping, she pulled away long enough to see Reagan's bloody jacket tied around his shoulder.

"What happened?" she asked, frowning at him.

"He got shot saving me," Reagan said, smiling.

She heard several people gasp. "Look at his feet," Cassey cried.

"I'm okay." He smiled at her, brushing a tear away from her face with his thumb. "As long as we're safe, everything's going to be okay."

Chapter Eighteen

Missy sat in the waiting room with Reagan and her family, waiting for Roman to get out of surgery. The bullet had lodged in his scapula and they had needed to get it out before it caused any more damage.

They were all sitting at the hospital just outside of Tallahassee. Roman's feet had been bandaged up and he'd been told to stay off his feet for the next few weeks.

Which, if she knew anything about him, would be a living hell.

"So," Cassey glanced over at her, "in all the excitement, we forgot to congratulate you."

She blinked and then frowned. "For?"

Cassey smiled. "Marrying our brother, of course."

Missy frowned. "I… We…" She shook her head. "We're not married."

Cassey smiled. "I heard the agent call you…"

Missy laughed, stopping her by shaking her head. "I just didn't think my business was any of his. We haven't married."

"Yet," Reagan added, causing everyone to chuckle.

"Well, we really wanted to be the first ones in the family to have kids," Marcus said, taking Shelly's hand in his, but it looks like you have us beat by eight years."

"What?" she gasped. "You're…" She looked between Shelly and Marcus, who just nodded.

She jumped up to hug him, just as the glass doors to the hospital shattered. She threw her body over Reagan's as glass flew everywhere. Then her arm was being yanked and she tightened her hold on her son as someone tried to pull him away from her.

There were a few moments of screaming and chaos as she and Reagan were pulled down a hallway. By the time things finally slowed down, she was staring up into caramel eyes so like hers she had to blink a few times to make sure she wasn't hallucinating.

"Well, well, little girl," her father said in a dry voice. "Looks like I finally got my hands on you again."

She recoiled just as his hand swung out and caught her just above her jaw. Stars exploded behind her eyes as she fell to the ground. Hearing Reagan cry out in pain, she pushed herself up from the ground just in time to see her father grab for the boy's arm.

"Don't you touch him," she growled as she threw herself at her father. She used every skill Roman had taught a sixteen-year-old girl who had been bullied and landed a solid kick to his shins.

Her left hook took the old man by surprise, causing him to drop the gun he had pointed at her son's head. The right cross landed on his left ear, causing him to howl with pain as blood sprayed from the open cut that appeared. Next, she gave two quick jabs and had him up against the wall. She wound her right back for one of Roman's specialty uppercuts, just as she heard the door behind them open. The blow landed on her father's chin, sending him sprawling to the ground just as her brothers rushed into the room, cheering her on.

She stood over her father as Marcus grabbed up the gun and held it at his head. "Don't you ever touch my family again, you bastard." She spit on the ground in front of him, then turned and snatched up her son and ran from the room, knowing her brothers would take care of the scumbag until the police arrived.

***

"I tell you," Cole said, laughing, "you should have seen it." He smiled over at Missy, pride showing clearly in his blue eyes. "She's a killer, that one."

"I've never seen a pro boxer fight like our little sister did," Marcus added, standing next to Shelly across the room.

Roman felt like a complete vegetable. His feet hurt like hell, and he couldn't even move his shoulder. He hadn't been there to protect his family when they'd needed it. His heart was heavy, knowing they could have been taken away from him so easily.

Missy's hand was in his as Reagan sat next to him on his hospital bed. The kid's eyes had been huge the entire time. A large smile played on his lips.

"Are you sure you're okay?" he asked her once more.

"Geez, Dad," Reagan said, rolling his eyes. He realized it would never get old, having the kid call him that. "Like Uncle Marcus and Cole said, Mom took out Grandpa like a pro. And she's promised me that she'll show me how to box like her." He smiled up at his mom and Roman saw something in the kid's eyes akin to hero worship.

"Well…" He reached over with his good arm

and ruffled the boy's dark hair. "You do know who taught her, right?"

Reagan smiled. "Sure, Aunt Cassey said she did."

Everyone in the room laughed as Cassey smiled and crossed her arms over her chest.

More than an hour later, after their family had left to go home, Missy tucked Reagan into the makeshift bed on the sofa across the room.

"He didn't want to leave," she said softly. "I hope it's okay with the hospital that we stay tonight."

He smiled and patted the spot next to him. "Just let them try to remove you." He chuckled. "From the sounds of it, you can hold your own ground." His smile fell away.

"What?" she asked, brushing her finger across his nose. "Why the sad look?"

His eyes met hers. "I wasn't there to protect you."

She smiled. "Oh, but you were. Who do you think taught me all those moves. If it hadn't been for you…" She shook her head and closed her eyes as he pulled her closer.

"Shhh, don't think about it," he whispered into her hair. "We're safe now." She nodded. "Besides, no more need to run," he said, causing her to pull back.

She smiled down at him and nodded. “Yes, no more running.”

“Does that mean you’ll come home?”

She sighed. “I am home.”

He nodded. “Then so am I.”

She shook her head. “No, not yet. You will be, once we make it official.” He frowned. “Our little sister was right about one thing.”

His eyebrows shot up. “Oh? Are you under the assumption that she taught you boxing?”

She chuckled and shook her head no. “No, but we should be married. I want to have the last name of Grayton one more time.” She smiled. “Marry me and”—she looked over at their sleeping son—“take us home once more.”

He smiled and pulled her closer. “I thought you’d never ask.” He kissed her and then pulled back. “I always knew I would marry you,” he said, brushing a tear from her face.

“Oh?” She smiled down at him. “How?”

He chuckled. “Because we met on your wedding day and I silently said my vows that day, standing on the shore of the lake.”

Tears rolled down her cheek. “What vows?”

“To cherish, protect, and love you til my dying days.” He pulled her down to a kiss and held onto her knowing that he’d do just that.

Last Resort – Preview

Prologue

She was running for her life. Knowing what she would see if she looked back, she kept her eyes trained forward. She tried to avoid roots or limbs that might trip her up, taking each step as carefully as she could at this speed. Her mind flashed to images of what she'd witnessed minutes before, yet she was oddly clear about what she needed to do for a seven-year-old.

Branches scraped her legs and arms as she ran, and her breath hitched with every step she took. Her ears were straining to hear if she was being chased, but she couldn't hear anything beyond her breathing and her loud heartbeat.

When she couldn't run any longer, she ducked behind a large tree and squatted until she was in a tight ball. She tried to slow her breathing down so she could listen, but it took forever to get her breath under control. She didn't hear the footsteps until a shadow fell a few feet from her.

Wrapping her arms around her knees, she waited for what she knew was coming. She was sure she knew what the outcome of the night would be, so nothing could have prepared her for what happened next.

"Are you all right?" a soft voice asked next to her.

Her head jerked up. Her long, dark, stringy hair

got in her face, so she shoved the strands away with her dirty hands.

She looked up and noticed the angel who stood over her. Everything about the woman was aglow; even the woman's clothes shined in the evening light. Her long blonde hair looked soft, softer than anything Cassandra had ever seen. The woman's hands were stretched out to her, and she could see gold rings on almost every finger.

"Here now, no one is going to hurt you anymore. Come with me, Cassandra. I'll keep you safe." The woman's soft voice almost mesmerized her.

Slipping her little, dirty hand in the woman's larger one, she sighed as she felt her soft, warm skin next to hers. She'd never experienced anything so soft in her life.

"How?" she whispered, looking around just in case. "How do you know my name?"

The woman shook her head. "I'll tell you in the car. Come on, we have to move; they're on their way here now."

Cassandra could hear them now. The sound was almost deafening to her tiny ears as her heart rate spiked. She bolted from her hiding spot and ran beside the woman.

The road, which she'd been told never to go near, was only a few feet from them, yet the limbs were thicker here and they had to fight their way through it. The woman's dress ripped as thorns pulled at it. Cassandra's legs and arms bled as deep scratches appeared on her skin.

Finally, they hit the clearing and the woman pulled open a car door.

"Quick, get in." She rushed around to the driver's door and jumped in.

Cassandra sat in the large front seat, her legs tucked up to her chest, her eyes glued to the trees, waiting, watching.

As they sped off, she sighed and her eyes slid closed for just a moment as she let her guard down. Then she opened them and looked at the woman.

"Who are you? How do you know my name?"

The woman smiled at her and glanced in the rear-view mirror.

"My name is Lilly. I'm your caseworker."

Cassandra's eyes were glued to her. "What is that?"

Lilly chuckled. "It's like a guardian angel." She smiled and put her hand over Cassandra's hair. Cassandra flinched away, not knowing what the gesture meant. She'd never been touched so softly before.

"What's a guardian angel?" she asked, sliding towards the door more.

"Someone who makes sure that you will never

be hurt again."

"How are you going to do that?" Cassandra got up on her knees and looked out the back window of the car, making sure they weren't being followed.

"By taking you somewhere where they can't find you. I know this place"—she smiled, looking down at her—"where kids like you can be safe."

Cassandra doubted there was a place like that. Looking out the window of the car as it traveled quickly down the dark road, she thought that there wasn't anyone out there like her. Especially not someone who had gone through what she had. She knew why she had suffered, why she'd been forced to do things she didn't want to—she was the devil's child. Or so her father and stepmother had told her for as long as she could remember.

Her stepmother, Kimberly, had entered her life when she was two. She didn't remember much from before that, but her father had told her that her mother, whom he described as an angel, had died giving birth to her. She had hoped that Kimberly's arrival would save her from the hell she was living—never leaving a ten-by-ten-foot cell—but she quickly learned that wouldn't be the case. This became very clear when Kimberly beat her that first week for stealing a piece of her bread.

As the car drove down the dark highway, Cassandra fell asleep, her little body tense even in sleep. She woke when they came to a stop.

"Sorry, I have to stop for gas. Would you like something to eat?" Lilly asked gently.

"Yes!" she thought. But she knew better than to answer an adult's question. Looking down at her hands, she shook her head.

"Well, I'm starving." Lilly's voice was so calm, it almost made Cassandra believe she could trust her. "You stay put. Promise me?"

Cassandra glanced at the woman. Her smile was so bright. Her blue eyes looked so kind. If ever there was an angel, Cassandra believed it was her caseworker, Lilly. Nodding her head, she looked back down at her dirty hands.

Lilly got out of the car, shutting the door gently behind her.

Cassandra didn't watch as she pumped gas; she kept her eyes and head down like she'd been taught. But when Lilly walked towards the little gas station, she picked her eyes up and glanced towards the building. After she saw Lilly walk through the doors, she looked around. This was a new place. It wasn't the gas station her father had stopped at. This was someplace she'd never been before. Her eyes got wide as she looked at the bright lights. There were large machines sitting right outside the doors.

Cassandra couldn't read well, so she didn't know what the red and white words said. She'd learned her colors from a book she'd had when she was four. Red was spelled R-E-D. She knew all the colors and often would close her eyes and remember every page of the small cloth book that her stepmother had burned one day when she'd been looking at it instead of sleeping.

When she saw Lilly walking back, she quickly ducked her head back down, looking at her dirty fingers. Then she noticed the dirt on the carpet of the car from her shoes. Jumping down, she quickly picked up the larger pieces and shoved them into her mouth and tried to swallow them.

"Here now," Lilly said, getting into the car. "What are you doing?"

"Nothing." She sat back up and prayed that the woman didn't see the dirt she wasn't quick enough to get.

"What do you have in your mouth?" Lilly asked.

"Nothing," Cassandra said again, looking out the window. Tears were streaming down her face.

"Cassandra, look at me, please." The "please" broke through her defenses, and she looked over at the woman.

"I'm not going to hurt you. No one is going to hurt you again. I promise. Now tell me what you have in your mouth, please."

"Dirt," she blurted out. "I'm sorry. I got dirt in your pretty car. I didn't…" She stopped talking and jumped away when Lilly reached over and touched her hand gently.

"Cassandra, look down here." She pointed to her side of the car. Dirt was all over the floor, even on her clothes. "I'm dirtier than you are, I think." She smiled at her and something shifted in Cassandra's heart.

"You…" She took a deep breath. "You aren't mad at me?"

Lilly shook her head. "No, honey. Now open your door and spit the dirt out. It must taste gross."

Cassandra did as she was asked. She'd learned long ago to always do what grownups told her to.

"Now, I bet this will taste a great deal better." She pulled a white bag between them. "I know it's not good to give children soda, but I think this one time we can make an exception." She pulled out a can that looked just like the machine she'd been looking at earlier.

"What is it?" Cassandra asked and then quickly tucked herself into a ball. She knew better than to ask questions. She must be tired to let her guard slip so much.

"It's okay, honey. You can ask all the questions you want. It's called a Coke. Would you like to try it?"

Cassandra nodded.

"I have a turkey sandwich and some potato chips here. I bought enough for you, just in case you got hungry. We still have a long way to drive before morning."

Cassandra looked at the sandwich. It was wrapped in a bag, and the chips were her favorite kind. She'd snuck one from Kimberly's large bag once and had gotten a whooping, but it had been worth it.

Lilly took out another sandwich and a bag of potato chips and started eating. Cassandra watched her for a few minutes, and then slowly reached over for the food. She wasn't starved. Her father had seen to it that she'd looked plenty healthy when the police showed up, but she was given only what she needed.

"*Kids don't need to eat much. After all, all you do is sleep and poop*," her father had told her over and over. She always thought there was something wrong with her because she wanted to go outside and play—to run in the dirt road, to jump off the tire hill that was in their front yard, or to just lay in the grass and watch the clouds go by.

She slowly opened the bag and took a bite of the sandwich. It was good. So good, she quickly ate every crumb. When Lilly opened the bag of chips for her, she ate every last one of those. Then she heard a noise she hadn't heard before and jumped.

"Would you like to try this?" Lilly held out the Coke can. Cassandra nodded and took the soda. She took a sip and her eyes slid closed. The bubbles ticked her nose and made her throat feel funny. She looked over at Lilly. Lilly had a smile on her face. “It’s good, huh?”

Lilly opened her own soda and drank from it. “Oh!” Lilly said, making Cassandra jump, spilling a little Coke on her clothes.

“I’m sorry.” She started frantically wiping the dark liquid off her dirty clothes.

“Honey, it’s okay. Don’t worry about it.” Lilly smiled at her. “I’m sorry for scaring you. I was just going to give you this.” She pulled out a package from the white bag. “They’re cupcakes.”

There were two circles in a clear package. Cassandra had never seen anything like it. They had white swirly lines across them. Reaching over, Cassandra took them from Lilly’s waiting hands.

“Thank you,” Cassandra said and sat them on her lap before taking another drink from her soda.

“Well, aren’t you going to eat them?” Lilly asked.

“They’re awful pretty,” Cassandra said.

Lilly laughed. “Yes, I suppose they are. Here, let me help you open the package.”

Lilly opened the bag and handed one circle to her. When Cassandra bit into it, the richness sank into every pore of her little body. She felt goose bumps rise on her arms and legs. The little hairs on her entire body stood straight up.

“What is this?” Cassandra asked, a smile on her face for the first time.

"Chocolate," Lilly said, smiling back.

The rest of the car trip, Cassandra looked out the dark window and thought about chocolate. How could she get more? Where would she get more? Was it something everyone had?

Her little mind finally ran out of questions, and she rested her head against the car door again. She woke when the car stopped suddenly. This time, the sun was just rising.

"Here we are," Lilly said in a cheerful voice. "Your new home."

The place was huge. Cassandra looked out the front window and instantly was afraid. It had three stories and was cleaner than anything she'd ever imagined.

"There are four other kids around your age living here now, but others come and go. You'll enjoy it here." Lilly got out of the car after honking the horn several times. She walked around and opened Cassandra's door, smiling the entire time.

Cassandra shrunk herself back into the car seat, holding the empty cupcake package tightly to her chest. She shook her head, no.

"I don't wanna stay here."

Lilly knelt down beside her. "It's okay, honey. No one is going to hurt you here. I promise you."

Shaking her head again, she watched as three

boys her age came running out the front door. Their clothes were clean and they had new shoes on their feet. Two had dark hair, one with blue eyes and one with dark brown eyes. The last boy had blond hair like Lilly.

Cassandra didn't know much about boys, but she knew they looked tough, and she didn't want to deal with them. She shook her head from side to side, faster.

"Look, here comes Marissa. She's your age and just arrived here last month."

Cassandra looked over just in time to see a girl around her age walk out the front door. She had a small kitty in her hands and was wearing a white dress and sandals. Her blonde hair was pulled back in short braids.

Cassandra looked at Lilly. "I know they have some chocolate in there and if you don't like it here, you can come home with me. Okay?"

Finally, Cassandra nodded and got out of the car, holding onto Lilly's hand as they walked up the front steps under the watchful eye of the four kids and four adults.

Cassandra didn't pay much attention to the kids since she knew the adults were the ones in charge. There were two women and an older man who looked frail. She knew she could outrun him if she had to. One of the women looked strong and capable; the other looked overweight and older. Cassandra knew that didn't mean she couldn't run fast since Kimberly had been pudgy and fast.

"Hi, everyone, this is Cassey." Lilly looked down and winked at her. Cassandra liked the shorter name; she'd always thought her name was too long and too big for her.

"Hi, Cassey," everyone said together.

"Cassey," Lilly said, smiling down at her, "this is Mr. and Mrs. Grayton. They own this house. And these are their daughters, Julie and Karen. Julie teaches school and will be responsible for you."

"Hello," she said under her breath.

"Hi," Julie said, kneeling down to her. Her hands were tan and she wore a faded pair of jeans and a button-up shirt with flowers on it. Her short brown hair was curly and looked soft like Lilly's. Her brown eyes looked rich and warm like the rest of her. "I've made some pancakes for breakfast. Would you like to come in and have some?"

Cassey looked up to Lilly and when Lilly nodded, she looked at Julie and said, "Yes, please."

Other books by Jill Sanders

The Pride Series

Finding Pride
Discovering Pride
Returning Pride
Lasting Pride
Serving Pride
Red Hot Christmas
My Sweet Valentine
Return To Me
Rescue Me

The Secret Series

Secret Seduction
Secret Pleasure
Secret Guardian
Secret Passions
Secret Identity
Secret Sauce

The West Series

Loving Lauren
Taming Alex
Holding Haley
Missy's Moment
Breaking Travis
Roping Ryan
Wild Bride
Corey's Catch

The Grayton Series

Last Resort
Someday Beach
Rip Current
In Too Deep

NEW Series
(Coming Soon)
Unlucky In Love
Sweet Resolve

For a complete list of books, visit *http://JillSanders.com*

This is a work of fiction. Names, characters, places, and incidents are either the product of the author's imagination or are used fictitiously, and any resemblance to actual persons, living or dead, business establishments, events, or locales is entirely coincidental.

ISBN: 978-1-942896-05-0

Copyeditor: Erica Ellis – inkdeepediting.com

About the Author

Jill Sanders is the New York Times and USA Today bestselling author of the Pride Series, Secret Series and West Series romance novels. Having sold over 150,000 books within 6 months of her first release, she continues to lure new readers with her sweet and sexy stories. Her books are available in every English speaking country and are now being translated to six different languages, and recorded for audiobook.

Born as an identical twin in a large family, she was raised in the Pacific Northwest. She later relocated to Colorado for college and a successful IT career before discovering her talent as a writer. She now makes her home in charming rural Florida where she enjoys the beach, swimming, hiking, wine tasting, and, of course, writing.

CPSIA information can be obtained
at www.ICGtesting.com
Printed in the USA
BVHW04s0830280318
511834BV00015B/269/P